The Satisfying Lie

A Novel

Tamika Lavette Shuler

The Satisfying Lie by Tamika Lavette Shuler

Copyright © 2008

Cover design by Lulu.

Printed in the United States of America

10 9 8

ISBN 978-0-6152-0618-9

Dedication

This book is dedicated to all the young women who are faced with learning self and the responsibility of life outside the cradle called home. May you be encouraged to find God in the midst of your discovery of your purpose of life.

Acknowledgments

Special thanks to the Great God above for the opportunities in life. I would like to thank my mother for a second, third, forth and many more chances. My entire family for their love and support through it all! I've learned to trust in God! To those of you who purchased my first official DRAFT unpublished, unedited, uncut version of *The Satisfying Lie* you helped me get to this point. You know who you are! Thanks a million! New journey's are ahead and I hope to see many on my way! Also, to many of my favorite authors who are still standing and encouraging me by your works!

Chapter One

She sat there alone in her room listening to the words she wrote flow off her tongue. The candlelight shadows danced on the wall to the beat of her song. All the blinds were closed in the room so that no light from the outside could enter. Her poster stared at her watching her every move and she stared back at it dreaming of the audience, the stage, and her song. She was an artist but she didn't paint pictures. She created characters that would cater to her needs-good or bad. This musical genius created shows bigger than Broadway but dangerous like a fight match. However, she was the only person left on the stage and she battled herself in the ring in the city. Her life was snatched from her but everyday she tried to resuscitate her dreams back to life. This girl never realized that the dead could not be raised. For every moment of pleasure she added a lifetime of pain that would one day end.

Marley promised herself she would never let Chicago take control of her. Sitting in a psychiatrist office twice a week made her realize that she made everyone's dreams in the big city come true except her own.

"It's amazing how my life changed in such a short period of time," she said.

"Would you like to tell me where your story began Marley?" asked Dr. Ross. For the past two months retelling her story is all she wrote. A broken dream was the case she gave herself. Fantasy is her name.

"Do you really want to know or are you just wasting my time Dr. Ross. See I am tired of wasting time in this place. Diagnose me as crazy, malicious, unstable, and depressed; whatever you want but my time is almost up and I am going to live my dreams. I have told my story to Dr. Johns and he said to me, Marley, I think you will be just fine. It's anxiety. I have told my story to Dr. Perry and she said Marley you have a bipolar disorder. A few pills a night and you will be just fine.

Now I have to rehash my story to you and what are you going to diagnose me as!" she screamed in a rage. It was that kind of outburst that let the psychiatrist know she wasn't ready to face the world that aided her to her current state of mind.

She has been in Vicente Psychiatric Ward for 3 months and continuously promises herself she will be leaving soon to live out her dreams. However, everyone else's opinion is different.

It began spring 2006 when she received a letter stating she had been accepted to attend college in Chicago, Illinois. Everyone in her family was so excited. She would be the first female in her family to attend a four year institution of higher learning. Marley and her friends always talked about attending college in a big city. Shania, her best friend since preschool, wanted to attend NYU and Deidre, her other friend, wanted to attended Howard University. There talks on the phone always ended with "I just want to get out of this small town!"

Their was one person, however, who was uneasy about Marley's choice of colleges-her grandmother. Mama Sheppard, as they affectionately called her, has seen many in her lifetime become the city life instead of living the city life. She knew her granddaughter was very intelligent but Mama Sheppard was too afraid that the streets would take her weak mind. Marley was the type of girl who dated guys that were considered "out of her league". Her boyfriends consisted of the guys who came from good families but they decided to do otherwise to prove something to the world.

Her time was spent standing on the corner with her girl-friends or walking up and down the block while the cars drove by beeping horns at their innocent beauty.

"Marley you need to leave that knuckle head Brown boy alone. He knows good and well his mama ain't raise him like that. He too far gone to change with his pants sagging below his behind. See y'all young folks think you know everything."

"Mama Sheppard please give me a break today. Damien is so cool. So what if he hangs out a lot. All the young kids do. And for your information Mama he goes to school and he is smart. We do our school work together and he wants to be a PE Teacher."

"When are you going to learn girl these boys will tell you anything to keep your mind going? That boy ain't thinking about shooting a basketball let alone wanting to teach someone else how to. You better open your eye's now Miss Marley if you talking about going to college in Chicago. Wish you would just stay home and make a difference in this community."

"But Mama Sheppard my dreams will be fulfilled in a bigger city. I am going to major in Music and join the school choir. I want to sing Mama. Let me have that one thing to live for. And like everyone else in the industry when I get big then I will come back and give to the community. Ok mama...just believe in me and I promise I won't let you down."

"Come give your Mama a hug. I just don't want you to fall short like so many do. Baby you are so smart and that's your weakness. You make sure you use your intelligence to make you strong and successful. And always pray, you hear me."

Marley shook her head to let her grandmother know she would do as expected of her. That was the last serious heart to heart talk she had with her grandmother.

Chapter Two

"Meet me at the laundry mat," the deep voice on the other end of the phone said. It was Damien and to hear his voice made her excited. Marley got dressed and headed down the street. She had a thank you card in her purse that she purchased earlier to let him know how much she appreciated him.

"So, you ready to head to Chi-town Ma," he asked.

"I wish you would have applied to school in Chicago so we could be together. Just like our favorite movie Love and Basketball," she said as she hugged him. He interrupted her never-let-me go hug with disturbing news.

"Look Marley. This long distance love isn't going to work. You will be a million miles away focused for the next 4 years of your life."

"Boy I'll be home so much you won't even notice I am away in school. And you know I got a lot of calling cards for graduation and I will call you every chance I get. It'll work ok," she said to him in her sweet innocent voice.

"This ain't easy but we have to end this. I want you to be happy and not worried about calling me and making sure I'm alright. Your happiness makes me happy. Girl you are going to be in a new place with new people. Go and do something. This has nothing to do with you. I promise you'll understand later."

"So, you want me to forget about you and us? Of course this isn't easy" cried Marley.

"No, I am not saying forget about me. I want you to call me and when you come in town we'll see each other. I just want you to go to school and do your thing Marley. Not many people get that opportunity, you know."

"No, I don't know but if this will make you feel better about me and us then I understand. When I get there I'm going to write my first song and dedicate it to you."

"So I am going to hear that beautiful voice on the radio one day?" asked Damien as he wiped the tears from her face.

"Just for you," she said.

"Come sing that song you always sing for me one more time," Damien said and she did just that.

The day came to pack up all her graduation gifts, clothes and memories. It was time to head out for school. She was excited with butterflies fluttering in her tummy. The drive was long and Marley thought the entire way of all the possible ways to be successful in Chicago with her music career. The thought of leaving behind so many people she loved made her shed a few tears but Marley knew she was making a good solid decision. Chicago would be different. She would be living off campus in an apartment owned by the university.

Two of her roommates had already settled in and were anxiously awaiting her arrival. They communicated on a weekly basis and this would be there first time seeing each other. She lay on her older brother's lap staring at the ceiling of the van thinking about her grandmother's words and her first love.

They finally arrived at the complex and she could see her room from the street. Her roommates made a sign that said "Welcome Marley" and hung it in the window.

"Look Mom! That's my room up there on the 4th floor!" she screamed with excitement.

She looked around and took in her first fresh breath of Chicago air not realizing that the very same breath she took would eventually suffocate her. The city was beautiful. There was a bookstore with a Starbucks attached. There were several side walk cafés and a small jazz club on the corner. People were walking up and down the street, cars were tooting horns through traffic, and there stood Marley ready for a new start of life.

"Welcome home Marley! Allow me to introduce myself. I am Felicia but everyone calls me Fe Fe and this is our other roommate Jessica. It's good to finally meet you."

"Same here. This is my brother Jamie, my mom, and last but not least, my daddy. The man who drove all the way here and listened to me sing a million and one songs for the University choir auditions next Wednesday."

"Can we help get anything else out the car?" asked Felicia.

She hailed from Philadelphia. Felicia was a freshman also who decided to attend college to get a taste of a new scene. A very beautiful round a way girl from the hood was how many described her. You could tell by her thick accent, tight jeans and her stance that she was an attitude carrying jazzy girl who took nothing less than what she had to give. She has seen a lot in her days in Philly and college seemed like the only way out. Felicia was very smart and used her street wisdom to get her a lot of places. Chicago was one of them. She already began checking out the life of Chicago and what it had to offer.

There was an orientation on campus for first year students that Felicia and Marley attended with her parents. The girls were bored to death as the president of the school spoke. Before leaving, he told the students to "look to your left and your right. The very same classmates you are sitting next to may not be here next year. Welcome freshmen. We hope you will make this experience educational as well as pleasurable." The students looked around at each other shrugging their shoulders and smirking, not realizing how serious the words would hit home for some.

Everything was unpacked, hammered to the wall, folded in the drawers and ready for the adults to leave. Her parents could feel the uneasiness settling in the room so they said their last goodbye's and parted ways, leaving their daughter in the hands of a new world. Marley was anxious to see the new scene and Felicia was ready to introduce her to it.

"So what's on the agenda for tonight ladies?" asked Marley. She was trying so hard to make herself available for whatever goes on with her roommates.

"Well it depends on a few things. First before we talk about going out we need to make sure there is a clear understanding of things around here," said Jessica. Miss Classy-I-Don't-Take-Anything-but-the-Best was on her way to the top. She hated the fact that she had to share an apartment with two females let alone two freshmen. However, she made up in her mind that she would take it easy on them because she too had to wear their shoes once. Jessica has lived in Chicago for 3 years. She transferred from the University of Miami as a sophomore, sat out a year to work an internship, and then re-entered college to major in something that she knew would make her wealthy-Entertainment Law.

There is one thing everyone says about her-she's going to the top some way some how. Once her mind is made up on something you don't have to worry about Jessica changing it for anyone or anything. She has seen the best of Chicago and even the worst and a bad experience something she vowed not to become.

"Ok ladies. We have all talked on the phone, emailed each other, and everything. Wonderful! But really there are a few things that we need to make sure we do to keep things smooth between everyone. Now let's first talk about our pet peeves. I can't stand a lot of people in the apartment late at night. Since we only have one bathroom, I think everyone should be considerate of others and clean after them. That really should apply to every shared room in the house. Ok well enough of me what about you Felicia. Is there anything you want to lay on the table?"

"Well I really don't have pets- I left my dog at home. Second of all, I'm not a petty person and besides I think it's common sense to do all those things. I think we need to let each other know our schedules because I like to play my music loud in the mornings to get me going and I don't want to wake anyone. Other than that I am pretty laid back and honestly once I meet a lot people you probably won't see much of me. I stay on the go."

"Well I guess it's my turn," said Marley. "Everything has been said. I am not a neat freak or anything. I just like things to look in order. That's all I guess."

"I don't know about y'all but I'm ready to get out right now." Felicia was the life of the house. She was into the whole hip hop culture from the way she talked to the way she dressed. Marley knew that with Felicia around there would never be a dull moment.

The girls got dressed for the night life and for Marley this too was a new experience.

It took forever for everyone to decide what outfit would turn heads that night. They knew since school was back in, there would be something to cater to their party needs. Jessica stepped out the bathroom looking like America's next top model. Her light pecan brown complexion sucked the gold dress that hugged every curve of her body. To accentuate her gear she wore shimmering gold stiletto heels and a gold Coach clutch bag. Her make up was freshly flawless. She was sure to get the attention she yearned for that night.

Felicia's scent yelled Philly all the way. Her hip huggers were etched in Red saying Ecko. Fitting her young upper body was an Ecko top. She wore her hair in a pony tail to the side with her make-up matching all the red stitching in her clothes. To bring out her small oval shaped face she wore big hoop earrings dangling to her shoulders with a signature F in the center. Her look said I am slender, sexy and ready to bring the pain if necessary.

And then there was Marley. She was naturally beautiful. She needed not one touch of make up to add to her beauty. Her lips had a natural pink tone that just needed a touch a lip glass. Marley really was not into to style like everyone else. Being from a small town fashion was not about name brand but looks. She wore tight Capris, a pink baby tee, and some thong sandals with a small heel.

"Marley where are you going with that on?" asked Felicia

"Girl you look like a model for Goody's or something. Step over here and let me help you out," said Jessica. By the time she rearranged a few strands of hair, blushed up Marley cheeks, and gave her a shimmering top to wear with her Capris she looked liked a brand new person.

The girls headed for the club. Each one turning heads from left to right as they walked down the busy streets. This was a new scene for Marley as she wasn't use to the vibrant youthful atmosphere. Felicia and Jessica on the other hand fit in well with the crowd.

Before Marley could turn to one of them to talk both girls were on the dance floor mingling with the crowd of college students.

Several guys approached Marley and each one she turned down. She scoped the area out from the flashing lights above to the shoes on the feet of the girl standing next to her. This country girl was in awe. She stood with her mouth literally gaped open. Marley never had a chance back home to taste the aroma of an upscale club scene. Taking hours to get stylish to dance and mingle was something no one back home did. She was use to girls wearing jeans and tank tops and guys in white tees and A-ones at block parties. Not saying anything was wrong with the down home atmosphere but this gave Marley a different view of the city life.

Felicia noticed Marley standing alone so she decided to bring the party to her. She took a few people she met with her to introduce them to Marley.

"Girl are you alright. You look like you are afraid to move."

"Fe Fe the place is so hot. I'm just amazed at all these people!"

"Well since you decided to just stand here I thought I'd bring the crowd to you. This is Mike and Ronnie. Y'all have to excuse my roommate but she isn't use to the city."

"So did Jessica get lost in the crowd" screamed Marley over the loud music.

"No, some guys she met invited her up to the VIP section. She said she'll come get us once she gets a feel of what they are about. Know what I'm saying?"

One of the guys invited Marley to dance and of course Felicia made sure she didn't turn him down. When it came to music Marley could hold the perfect tune but moving her body was another story. Mike could tell she was a little uncomfortable so he gave her a drink.

"Ugh. What is this?" she asked after she took a sip of the mysterious drink.

"Girl try this. It's called a Twist. Loosen up and get yo dance on!" yelled Felicia over the loud music.

"Ok now I have had some of this before. I'll take this instead."

Marley gulped down the tube of hypnotic and went for a few more. She would soon realize that she was in another world.

The girls went up to the VIP room and Marley was feeling a whole lot better. If you didn't know her you would have thought she was a regular club hopper. She went from being the quiet country girl to the center of the VIP room. It was a side Felicia was glad to see and a side Jessica knew would eventually come to the surface.

"I thought you said you could hold your alcohol" yelled Jessica as she helped Felicia carry Marley up the stairs. By the time the party was over Marley had a large consumption of Hypnotic and shots of Tequila. Jessica was not a heavy drinker and Felicia's preference was smoking.

"We will not be doing this again Miss Marley," said Felicia. "Now you need to get it together because we have another flight of stairs to go up!"

As they got in the apartment Marley threw up all over the floor and the girls screamed, "Dang!" in unison. Jessica pushed Marley in the tub and filled it up with cold water and Felicia scrubbed the vomit covered floor while the incense burned and her music bumped.

The girls tidied up the apartment and put Marley in the bed. As Felicia turned off the light she yelled, "this is the last time!"

Chapter Three

A few weeks of school came and went with the blink of an eye. Marley was exhausted by the time the weekend came. She woke up Saturday morning and called her parents. Her mother was so excited to hear from her. The first thing she told her mother about was the audition for the university choir. Her audition went well. She even landed the solo parts for several concerts to come. This girl was talented with her voice. She never sang on the church choir but she always entered talent shows and was placed first in each one.

"I was so nervous when I went in the audition but once I started singing I felt better."

"So how are your classes and your professors?" her mother asked. She really wasn't interested in the audition. Her mother always told Marley she was aiming for a hopeless future in Music and wished she would focus her time on something that was promising like education or medicine.

"I like my classes. I just have to get use to my schedule. It's not like high school when we go for the whole day. My last class is Biology and we get out at 6:45."

"Well you just stay focused on your school work and you'll be fine. We are about to head to Mama's house for breakfast. Your daddy had to work this morning so he's going to miss his salmon patties."

Marley missed her family as she was use to spending Saturday mornings at her grandmother's house. On Saturday morning her entire family-aunts, uncles, and cousins-would eat breakfast at Mama Sheppard's.

"Well Ma. I'll be home for fall break. Tell everyone I love them and miss them dearly," she said as she ended the conversation. She was trying to save her phone card minutes for another person she missed-her ex boyfriend back home, Damien. Her parents thought she stopped talking with him when she left for school but she couldn't go another week without calling him. And of course they would never know who she called on her calling cards. She missed when she used to tell her parents she was going to the mall or walking to the corner store only to end up in the arms of her love. Damien told her it was going to be hard maintaining a relationship with her living in the big city. She wanted it to work and she knew she could get him back if she wanted to. That's when she decided to pick up the phone and call him.

After speaking with his mom she received some upsetting news. Her grandmother was right about Damien but Marley was too blind to see it. It wasn't that he was a bad person it was the fact that Marley changed her ways to please him. She would lie to her parents all the time on her whereabouts. One time her parents thought she was on a field trip with a local girls club. She doctored up a false permission slip and when her parents forgot to sign it she had one of her friends older sisters call the house acting concerned. Her parents let her go and they never found out the truth. She would go to the extreme when it came to deceiving others for Damien and her grandmother was the only one who could see right through her. She wanted no one to figure out the young deep connection she and Damien had. Marley thought as long as she strived hard to make Damien happy he would always be with her. Damien told Marley whatever she wanted to hear. He had no intention of being who Marley thought she wanted him to be.

To Damien as long as he was able get what he wanted it satisfied him. He was young and the neighborhood belonged to him. All the younger boys wanted to be just like him. He was a very clean cut young guy who stayed ahead of the latest fashion. You could see his deep yellow toned skin a mile way. His face was always shaved neatly and his hair had deep waves that would take you to any shore on the face of this earth. His cool personality would charm any woman young or old but his attitude was horrible. It was his rough attitude and charming personality that kept Marley chasing him since the summer of her junior year. Damien wanted Marley to get away from him but she would never understand the true reason and after receiving the disturbing news from his mother she still did not understand why but vowed to get her song on the radio just for him. It bothered her because she wasn't able to do anything to help him. All she could hear was her grandmother telling her "that boy ain't no good."

"What's wrong Marley?" asked Jessica.

"I don't know. I mean I do but I just don't know how to handle the news I just received from my boyfriends' mother."

"I didn't know you had a boyfriend. What happened?"

"I don't know that's the problem. If Damien is ever in a bind he knows to call me and now I don't know what happened. We are on hold relationship wise right now but I don't want anyone else. No one loves me like he does." She cried.

"Well I wish I could tell you what to do. Everything will be fine. It may not be as bad as you think. Is he away in school or something?"

"No. he actually decided not to go to school. I should've listened to my grandmother when she told me to go to school in my hometown. I would be closer to him. I wish I would've never left. Things probably would be different."

"Don't think like that. Girl you are in a new city, with different people, different places, and different things. Worrying is not going to help you. Just relax. You are here for a reason," said Jessica as she closed the door behind her.

Thinking about Damien made Marley homesick and tears streamed down her face the more she thought about how much she missed everyone. She fell asleep thinking to herself "am I ever going to see him again..."

Marley woke up and heard two screaming voices in the other room. She arose to see what was going on. As she walked in the front room she saw Jessica and Felicia in the kitchen arguing about the bathroom. Jessica was very particular about cleanliness and Felicia was the type of person to take care of some thing when it started bothering her. With their two personalities Marley knew it would not be long before this happened.

"Felicia all I am saying is that if you are going comb your hair over the sink clean it up after you finish. You have make up, hair, earrings and everything else all over the counter!" screamed Jessica.

"You woke me up 8 o'clock this morning to tell me about some make up and a few strands of hair. I don't have class until 2:30 today! Girl you could have moved my stuff over and handled your business!" yelled Felicia forgetting it was the weekend. Before they could keep the scream match up Marley and Jessica laughed at Felicia.

"What is so funny?" asked Felicia. "I do not have time for this crap this morning!

"Girl it's Sunday morning. You must have had a long night Felicia!" said Marley. "I need to clean up my room while y'all are in here arguing about cleaning up."

"Oh so you got jokes. It's Sunday for real?" asked Felicia.

"I don't care if it's Tuesday or Friday. I know somebody better get that mess up soon," said Jessica with a disgusted look on her face.

"Always trying to act like somebody's moms. Love you too! You girls should have been to the spot last night. It was popping hard in there. Guys were coming from every corner buying drinks like crazy. I just got home like 6 this morning and two hours later Jessica bust in my room raising hell about some hair."

"Felicia now you know that bathroom counter has been looking like that since your class on Tuesday. We all had this discussion when we first moved in here," said Jessica.

"Whatever. I'll do it when I get up later. I'm tired," Felicia said as she walked towards her room. For someone who was tired she sure did have her music loud.

"That girl is a mess," said Jessica. "I don't know what we are going to do with her. She and Marley just laughed as they begin cleaning the kitchen.

"Going on a mail run since no one has checked the mail in days" said Marley as she closed the door. She rarely received mail unless it was something from campus housing regarding the various campus activities but today to her surprise there was a letter address to Marley Denise Sheppard from her cousin Yolanda. She began reading the letter looking for juicy gossip about things going on back home.

Dear Marley:

Girl long time no hear. I hope you are still alive since you can't call your cousin. Your mom gave me your address so I decided to just drop a line. Things really haven't changed back home. Same old stuff. Auntie Janie and her new husband were arguing last week at breakfast and you know Mama Sheppard put a stop to that real quick. Oh Lacy is coming home from the service finally! She called momma last night with some drama of course about her baby daddy! Girl you know how that went! I can't wait to see my nephew. He is getting huge! Any ways, enough on the family how are things with you? Have you talked to Damien lately? Well I don't know how things are between you two but there are some things going on around the block about him. I just wanted to give you a heads up. I don't get in his business like that because you know I don't care much for him but you are like my sister and you know you deserve much better. Just call him and find out what's what then call me later. I am about to study for my quiz so hit me back. Or email me you know the information.

Love your long lost and only twin sister
Yolanda

As Marley went back in her apartment she folded up the letter and thought about what could be wrong with her Damien. The letter seemed to let Marley know that it could be bigger than what she assumed.

"So Marley, how are you doing? Being so far away from home I know it's hard adjusting to this big city."

"I ain't even going to lie. It's hard but I guess the more I get out the more people I'll meet. Honestly, I would prefer not to meet a lot of people, especially girls."

"Why do you say that?" asked Jessica.

"My teacher gave us our lab schedules and partners. That's the worse part about the class-my partner."

"Please say you don't have Dr. Gillespie with his flirty-self," said Jessica.

"Girl he is so cool. My partner is this chick who stares in the freaking mirror all day and flings her hair over her shoulders. How about our lab is at 5:30. Why she ain't show up for lab or class the next session."

"Ask for another partner. That's bad news already!"

"No this is what tripped me out. We had to exchange numbers in class. So I called the number that she gave me since she missed class and guess what she tells me."

"Oh lord here comes the drama!"

"You right! She said don't call her about some class she missed like I'm her momma and if she doesn't come to class why should I give a you know what!"

"I probably would've told you the same thing though."

"Why? I was just trying to make sure she was ok. I mean we are lab partners."

"But that ain't the point Marley. Girl we are in college. You are grown. If you don't go to class so be it. You don't have to answer to momma or daddy anymore. In this life you now have to worry about yourself."

"I guess the freedom part hasn't hit me yet," said Marley.

"Are you feeling a little better today?"

"I slept on it. But I guess this comes with the package of moving away from the people you care about. It's funny how you think you meet the right person and you give so much to see it work only for that person to tell you to move on or something forces you to move on."

"Yeah I know that feeling. Before I came back to Chicago I was engaged. Girl he was something else not to mention someone else's."

"For real Jessica. What happened?" asked Marley as she sat on the counter very attentive.

"To make a long story short and keep the memories back there. He was paid, he was sharp and he was married. Girl we use to go to the Bahamas on the weekends like it was down the street from my parents' house."

"How did you find out?"

"Girl I did not find out, she found me. All the questions had been asked and answered and all hell broke loose. So I left and that was that."

"Man that's a trip. Have you heard from him since?"

"Girl yes! He still calls but I can't even get close to him anymore. Too much drama."

"I hear that. Well I have to get to the library so I can study for this History test. Professor Kyushu is tough."

"Alright Marley. I'm here if you need to talk or vent."

Marley looked at Jessica in a different way since their small talk. It was the first time they ever sat down for girl talk. When she first met Jessica she thought she was an uppity city girl who was all about money, cars, and clothes, especially the night they went out for the first time. However, looking back on that night and after speaking with Jessica, Marley realized that she was a very focused young woman. Jessica was indeed a very classy chick with one thing in her view-dollar signs. She was not a money hungry girl but she came from a very wealthy family and she knew was nothing but the best. You could see it in her walk, in her talk and in her appearance. She did not hang out with drama queens or "hood" rats. Actually she did not have a strong click of "friends" because she had no time for extra baggage. She felt it would hold her back or block her vision and in Jessica's words "No one or nothing will stop [me] from getting to the top" and she meant that. Even if she had to push people out her path she was determined to make it to the top. For the first time in her life Marley was in the presence of a young determined female. She made up in her mind she had to adopt that same attitude to make it in her music career.

Chapter Four

Marley walked to campus alone. She knew if her father knew that he would have a fit. He preached so much to her about being alone on the streets of Chicago. She was standing at the crosswalk in front of the campus when two guys walked up behind. She glanced over her shoulder to see what they looked like in case anything happened and she recognized one of the guys from one of her classes. He too noticed her familiar face and decided to strike up a conversation.

"Aren't you in my biology class on Mondays?" asked the guy.

Marley looked him up and down and shook her head yes. She was actually lying just to get him off her back.

"Red bone acts like she's too good to speak. What's wrong with these girls around here," said the other guy. In Marley's eyes they both appeared to be a bunch of nobody's so she let the comment ride and began walking towards campus.

"Hey. Please excuse my roommate. He's what they call a dumb jock. I'm sorry if he offended you in any kind of way," said the classmate of Marley.

"No offense taken. I don't have time for stupidity. I'm Marley by the way and we don't have Biology together. It's history."

"My bad. I have big load this semester so you have to excuse my wrongness. I just know a familiar face when I see one."

"And who are you?" asked Marley.

"I'm Marcus. This is my second semester here and I am a Business Major with a minor in international business."

"Well it's nice to meet you Marcus. I hope you study hard for our test tomorrow. I'm on my way to the library so I guess I'll see you bright and early in class."

"Oh crap! That is right. Do you mind if I join you for a quick study session?"

"Actually I do mind. I really want to take this time to make sure I focus on some other things. So I'll see ya tomorrow in class."

"Sure thing," he said.

Marcus hurried back to his roommate with a disappointing look on his face. Today was not the day to make a move on Marley. Her attention was somewhere else unimaginable. Marley could feel their eyes following her as she disappeared in the crowd on campus.

She headed for the library to study but for some reason a very uneasy feeling came over her. As she sat at the table flipping through her notes and her study questions she began thinking about Damien. Her eyes flooded with tears as she reminisced on their good moments and their not so good moments. She realized how much this guy meant to her. It's amazing how this young girl had such a great passion to see him happy.

Marley would go above and beyond to show Damien her loyalty to him and only him. Thinking hard on what they had she could actually hear him saying "go and be something..." and that replayed in her mind the entire duration of her study session. She tried her hardest to focus on her test but her mind was on something else. While she laid her head on the table she wrote a letter to him.

When returning to the apartment Marley was hit with more disturbing news. Her father left a message with Felicia saying Mama Sheppard was very ill and since entering the hospital her health worsened. This was the bad feeling that overcame Marley at the library. She tried to call her parents to tell them she wanted to come home but she got no answer.

Mama Sheppard was very special to Marley. She helped Marley's mom raise her while her father was in the military. While her mother worked her grandmother kept, fed, spanked and nurtured her. She remembered laying on Mama Sheppard's bouncing knee as she sucked her thumb and Mama smacked her back. Looking back when she was home she could see it as if it happened yesterday. Mama Sheppard would holler down the street from her mailbox to call Marley and her cousin Yolanda "get y'all tails in this yard now. Off that street corner like y'all selling cookies. Ain't no Sheppard girls belong outside this gate. Ain't nobody but that Marley with her sneaky self. Catch ya down there one more time and you gone wish you would've stayed home with ya mama's!" Those were her exact words. Marley laughed as she reminisced on growing up with Mama Sheppard. Those same tears of laughter turned into tears of pain. She has not even spoken to Mama Sheppard since she's been in school. The very person who raised her and knew her from head to toe was very ill. "How could I be so selfish" Marley thought to herself as she realized she had not communicated a simple hello to her grandmother. She called her cousin Yolanda to see how things were back home since she was unable to reach anyone else.

"Marley," Yolanda cried, "Mama is not responding. Your daddy tried to call you to tell you he is sending for you on the next bus home."

"Yolanda what's wrong with Mama?" asked Marley as she packed her bag.

"I don't know. When all the grandkids were standing at her bedside she called your name Marley and after that she fell into a coma. You need to call your daddy. This is the number to the hospital" said Yolanda as she gave the information to Marley.

Marley called the hospital and was able to speak to her father. He told Marley the information to get to the bus station and how long it would take for her to get home. She dropped the phone and headed for the bus station rushing everyone and everything as if she was a hero going to save the day.

Chapter Five

When Marley arrived home she was hit with more bad news. Mama Sheppard closed her eyes for eternity. The first thing she thought of was Mama Sheppard calling for her. The first person she saw was her cousin Yolanda and they both hugged and cried together. Marley began thinking to herself "what did Mama have to say to me". Everyone in the neighborhood stopped by Mama's house to say goodbye and mourn with the family. She was well-respected in her community. There was not one person who did not come to her for something. Mama was blessed with an abundance of spiritual gifts. Everyone came to her for advice, for prayer, and numerous other things. She practically raised the entire block from the young to the one's having mid-life crises. This was a great loss for the neighborhood but a bigger loss for the family, especially Marley.

While home many of her friends visited but she really wanted to see one person-Damien. Although she was home to bid farewell to her grandmother, Damien stayed on her mind heavily. Marley was hoping that he would stop by or call or even send for her but he didn't. On the day of the wake she decided to pay him a visit.

"Hey Candy is Damien home?" she asked as she approached the lady on the porch. It was Damien's aunt who always sat on the porch from dusk to dawn.

"No Baby he ain't here. He's somewhere round the block," she said in her raspy voice as she smoked her cigarette. "Sorry to hear bout your grandma. She'll be missed greatly."

"Thanks. I know I sure will miss her. She meant a lot to me."

"She meant a lot to everybody. You'll never find another like her. Dame left bout 30 minutes ago. You can wait with me or gone round the block to find him."

"I think I'll just sit with you for a few minutes," she said in hopes he would return soon.

"How's school going in that big city? You know I use to live in Chicago for a while. I loved it."

"I like it too. It's different from here I'll tell ya. It's so big. I swear if I didn't stay around the block from campus I would get lost."

"You just be careful in that big city. It's a lot of slick-sters waitin' for young girls like you. If you ain't careful you'll turn into the streets taking everyone for a ride and forgettin' the true reason you came to the city."

"Why do you say that Candy?"

"Chile anybody can smell a fresh piece of bait like you and so many of those girls who come from all over the place. You got to keep your eyes on your prize or you'll be winnin' the race for the wrong reasons. You know who told me that before I left. Mama Sheppard. God rest her soul"

"You're scaring me now," said Marley as she listened attentively.

"I ain't the one to scare you. I'm just giving you some wisdom. See y'all still babies in the game. Look at my nephew. Now he wishes he would've listened to me."

"Maybe it ain't my business but what happened to Damien since I've been gone."

"You have to ask him but don't you give your heart to anyone who can't hold it. I know you call him and now you want to see him but you need to stay on top of your visions and stop letting your heart cloud your road to success."

"All I know is that I truly love Damien and I am going to school for me but my dreams are going to come true for us," said Marley as the advice went in one ear and out the other. She listened hard but hardly paid attention to the message. To Marley all that was encouraging but in her eye's it would "never happen to me, whatever happened to her" she thought to herself. Just as she was standing up to say good-bye to Candy she noticed a familiar face coming down the sidewalk. The site of that face made her eyes light up and she dashed off the porch to meet him at the gate. However, to her surprise the guy approaching the gate was not so happy to see her.

"Baby what's wrong. You look like you just got into a fight," she said not knowing if she should show how excited she was to see him or sympathy for his physical condition. Damien approached the yard and gave Marley a get-out-of-my-face look that would kill anyone's worse enemy.

"Is this not a good time Damien?" asked Marley. Still he paid her no attention and just walked right past her.

"Damien!" she cried. "What is wrong with you?" she asked following him into the house.

"How you going to just show up at my house without me knowing. You know I don't get down like that. When you start doing stuff like that!" he yelled at her hysterically.

"What do you mean? I just thought I would stop by to see you. I mean I wanted to talk to you especially with every-thing going on with my family now. I just needed to get away." She began crying. Marley knew something was wrong with Damien but she also knew that she never came around his house unless he called for her. She assumed since she was burden with her grandmothers death Damien would allow this exception but she failed to understand there was never any exceptions with Damien. And even with her grandmother's passing sympathy would not excuse her actions. For the first time she was able to experience the other side of Damien. Damien had his reasons. He was a secretive person and with all the trouble he just got out of there was no one or nothing that would bring any more heat than he could take.

"You need to leave Ma. I'll get up with you later," he said as he pushed her toward the door.

"Why are you trying to get rid of me? What are you do-ing so that you can't even speak with me for a minute!" she screamed at him "Now my grandmother passed away and you can't even hug me or talk to me." She walked around him toward his room only to find a young lady lying in one of the beds in his room.

"Get out!" screamed Damien as he pulled her so hard he popped her strap on her tank top. "You don't run nothing 'round here with your college brains. Go home and if I want to see you I'll call you later. You know better than that Ma. Dang!" he said as the screen door slammed behind her.

"You be good Marley and tell ya mamma I said hey," said Candy as Marley left the yard.

She had never seen him that angry but at the same time she had never done anything to make him that angry. Marley was hurting from her grandmother's death and also from what just happened but she was also confused. She wondered to herself who was the girl in his room. But she brushed it off knowing "Damien wouldn't do this" to her. "I'm just jumping to conclusions," she said to herself.

She went back to her grandmothers' house where everyone was looking at pictures, laughing, and sharing stories of Mama Sheppard. Marley couldn't believe the atmosphere of joy. Looking around at everyone and their cheerfulness made Marley so upset she began crying and screaming. She couldn't understand what everyone was so happy about. To her this was supposed to be a mourning session and it appeared to Marley everyone forgot their purpose for gathering. This was the first death in which Marley took in all the memories of someone close to her and turned it into a dispirited gathering. She went in her grandmothers' bed and held her pillow that Mama kept in her bed just for Marley. They were indeed close and Mama knew Marley's actions before Marley could make them into thoughts. Sitting in Mama's room, Marley could smell her grandmothers' mother scent. She could see her grandmother sitting in her rocking chair humming. She could feel her grandmothers touch stroking her as she cried. Mama Sheppard's presence was still in the air. The one thing that calmed Marley down was when she heard Mama Sheppard's voice. Mama told her "get up Marley. You are beautiful and don't you let anyone change that. You take your troubles to the Lord on your knees and you get up with faith. When the road gets too tough pump your brakes and when the wind gets too fierce adjust your sails. Remember baby that what don't kill you will mak you strong."

Marley was awakened by her cousin Yolanda telling her Damien wanted to see her down the block. She snuck out the back door and met Damien on the corner near her parents' house.

"Look Ma," he said as he held her tightly, "everything ain't peachy round here. A lot of things happened since you been gone and a nigga ain't been right since."

"Damien I didn't mean to upset you earlier. I just really needed to see you especially in my time of need."

"I am sorry to hear about your grandmother. I know you were very close to her."

"Damien I don't want to talk about that right now. Tell me what is going on with you?"

"I know you're wondering who that girl was in my room. That's Danielle from JW's high school. Marley she had a baby boy about 5 months ago. She and her folks had a little falling out and she didn't have a place to go. I could not just let her stay anywhere especially not with my son."

"Your son!" she screamed. Marley could not believe what she was hearing. Damien and Danielle had a son while she was away in school. Not to mention they messed around while she was dating Damien.

"I didn't mean to hurt you. I ain't ever told you a lie and I wanted to make sure I told you before you heard it from anyone else. We both made mistakes in the past and I just hope you can forgive me for this one."

"I'm just confused and a little hurt."

"Come here Marley. You will always be my number one girl. Always," he said as he held her tight. For the first time in Damien's life he really felt the connection Marley always spoke of. The average girl would have left him standing on the corner alone as they tried to pick up the pieces of their broken heart. Marley was not the average girl. She stayed there in his arms taking it all in. See, Marley was not upset over the fact that Damien was with Danielle. In fact her hurt had nothing to with the cheating. She longed for the day to be in Danielle's shoes. Marley wished it was her in the bed waiting for Damien to come while their son was out with his grandmother. She was hurt because it was not her.

"Damien why do I not hear from you? I just want to know that you are ok."

"I ain't going nowhere unless you forget your reason for going to Chicago-do not let a year pass by without getting your voice on the air."

"One year?" she asked. "That's too short of time."

"Thinking like that will have you chasing your dreams for the rest of your life. Girl you can blow. Tell me you can't."

"Whatever," she said as she laughed. She was happy to be with him. For Marley that's all that mattered. "I just can't picture you being somebody's daddy and changing diapers."

"Oh you got jokes!" he laughed as he kissed her on her forehead. He loved her truly and she loved him back even more.

Chapter Six

Marley did not attend the funeral. After she slept in her grandmothers' room that night she began saying "Mama Sheppard's not dead." She went back to school the day of the funeral but before she left she dropped her letter to Damien in the mail.

Marley was actually happy to be back in Chicago. She missed the fresh air, the busy streets and the crowded campus life. But most of all she missed her freedom. She was actually beginning to enjoy the freedom and the responsibilities that came along with it.

Felicia was home when she got back. She unpacked her pictures of her grandmother and other memorabilia she picked up from her Mama's house. Everyone felt Marley was not in good condition to return to school so soon and some even felt it was disrespectful for her not to bid farewell to her grandmother. To Marley her grandmother was not dead. And she needed to get back to the place where her dreams would come true for her....and her man.

Just as she was getting ready to rest for a while there was a knock at the door. It was Eric, one of Felicia's friends. Marley let him in and went to get Felicia.

"Fe Fe, Eric is here for you," she said as she went in Felicia's room where Miss Thang was getting ready for a hot date.

"Girl you look nice. I love the red highlights."

"Marley I didn't know you were home. How are you girl?"

"I am fine. My grandmother passed away before I got home and the funeral was today, but I decided not to go. To me, Mama Sheppard ain't dead in my heart."

"I'm sorry to hear that. You know I'm here if you need me," said Felicia as dressed for her date with Eric. She met him at one of the local hip hop spots. But she also had a friend she kicked it with heavily on campus. She prepared Marley for any phone calls or visits and Marley vowed she would relay the message to anyone that "Felicia went home for the weekend. I'll tell her to call you."

"There you go girl. We'll sit down and talk once I return tomorrow," said Felicia as she went out the door. Marley finally was able to lie down and get some rest. Felicia and Jessica were both gone for the rest of the night. It was Marley's first time alone in her apartment. She enjoyed the peaceful silence throughout the room. As she lay in bed she thought of the time she was able to spend with Damien. Although they were not physically together she felt proud to be his number one girl. She knew that he meant it from his heart.

The phone startled Marley thoughts. Her mind was somewhere else in the past. But reality would soon bring her up to speed. Forgetting what she and Felicia just talked about she quickly picked up the phone.

"Hey Troy."

"Who this, Marley."

"Yep...Yep. What's going on son?" she asked jokingly.

"So you got jokes on the NY lingo. Where Fe at?"

"She went out. She'll be back tomorrow. I'll tell her you called."

"Who was with her?" asked Troy. He and Marley had two classes together and he was the guy Felicia was seeing on campus. Marley and Felicia would go to his place from time to time and chill with the fellas but Marley did not know that Troy liked Felicia.

"I don't know dude name but they'll be back tomorrow. I think you might know him. I can't remember seeing him at the spot but you would know him if you see him." said Marley totally forgetting about what Felicia asked of her. She looked at her clock and set it to wake her in the morning at 7am. She had choir rehearsal at 9am.

The fall concert was in less than a month and Marley had practice 4 days out of the week instead of the usual two. She would visit Mr. Jackson, her concert choir director, during her spare time on campus. She loved the attention she received from him regarding her voice. Even when she needed a tune up he still continued to praise her. He loved her voice and knew the perfect person to match her with.

While walking to practice, Marley bumped into Marcus.

"Hey Marley. How's it going?" said Marcus. He was glad to see her. Now that he knew who she was he made it his business to speak to her when he ran into her and sometimes they would walk to lunch together. He was beginning to like Marley. There was something about her that attracted him to her. When he talked about Marley he would tell the guys "she is a very attractive sweet girl. And man she can sing too."

"Hey Marcus. What's up buddy?"

"Not too much going on. Just got finish working out with my roommates. I want to try out for the track team this semester. Tryouts are in November."

"Ok. I ain't mad at you trying to get your little workout on. Do your thing Marky Mark." She laughed with him.

"Oh this week I am Marky Mark. Last week I was Marco. Now what is it gonna be next week."

"We'll see how you act. So what are you about to get into? I got rehearsal in 10 minutes, but if you're not busy later on I was thinking we could walk to Blockbuster."

"Oh yeah we have to watch that video for History by next week. Ok that's cool. Just call me when you get back or better yet come by the dorm." He yelled as they parted separate ways.

Chapter Seven

There she stood with her beautiful stage presence as the choir hummed as back up. Her voice carried through the audience and brought tears to the surface of many onlookers. Marley held soulful tunes that took you back to the days of Billy Holliday stealing the hearts of many. When Marley auditioned for the university choir she immediately received the solo part for the fall concert. Mr. Jackson was so impressed with her ability he began working with her after rehearsals to prepare her for many events to come.

"Marley you did a spectacular job," said Dr. Kyushu who attended the show faithfully each fall.

"Girl I did not know you had a voice like that!" yelled Felicia. "I am so jealous. How about when you make it let me be your dancer. You know I can pop lock, Harlem shake it to the window and the wall."

"Marley Denise Sheppard. I can't say enough. You amaze every time. Here these are for you," said Marcus as he handed her a bouquet of fresh roses. He had a thing for Marley and everyone knew. But who could blame him after tonight.

"Oh Marcus these are so beautiful. You shouldn't have. I thought you were not going to make it because you had a meeting."

"All that matters is I made it in time to hear you. Dang girl you look fantastic!"

Marley blushed with a twinkle in her eyes as he stared deeply at her beauty. She did indeed look wonderful. Her black dress sparkled in the dim lighting of the concert hall. It fit her perfectly.

"Well I see you two have something up your sleeves so I'll leave you alone," said Felicia.

They laughed at her as she walked out the door being silly. As Marley and Marcus walked out the concert hall,

Marley was stopped by yet another fan, one who would give her something that added more to her life.

"Excuse me Miss. Sorry Bro, don't mean to cut between you two," he said to Marcus. "Your choir director asked me to come out tonight and I must admit I wasn't going to but I'm glad I did. I was just telling my partner I've never heard anyone like you."

"Thanks for coming out. I'm Marley and this is my friend Marcus. I didn't catch your name."

"Oh my bad. I'm Dre and this is my partner AJ. We are always in Chicago and we do a lot of work with Mr. Jackson. I just wanted to check you out and let you know you did a good job on that stage tonight. Hopefully I'll be seeing you for some upcoming things Mr. Jackson has lined up."

"Nice meeting you Dre and AJ," said Marley as she grabbed Marcus's hand and walked away.

Dre stood there as he watched his new star disappear into the Chicago night. She is destined for great things he said to himself and he knew he could be the one to make it happen.

Marcus took Marley out to dinner that evening at one of Chicago's finest dining places. After dinner they walked down the sidewalk shoulder to shoulder hand in hand feeling like the best two people in town. Marcus enjoyed Marley's company because it gave him a chance to get to know her personally. Often times they would meet for lunch on campus or at the library to chat. They would be seen in the park together just walking, talking and laughing. He felt like a real gentleman when he was around her. He believed she deserved the best that he could give. There was nothing he wouldn't do for her. He would put forth a lot of effort to show her how much he cared even when he couldn't afford it.

They arrived back at Marley's apartment and they both fell on the couch at the same time.

"This has been an evening full of events. I never thought in a million years I would be singing a solo part in the schools choir!" she said.

"Well I never thought in a million years that I would be listening to the next best thing to Mary J. Blige. Girl you did your thang tonight."

"It's nice to know you put me so high on the charts" she chuckled. "I can't recall the last time someone paid attention to me like you do. You know Marcus, I am so glad I met you. You really mean a lot to me, more than you think," she said as she leaned forward and kissed him. As she began to caress him he stopped her in her tracks.

"Marley, look, we don't have to do this," he said. "I want you to know you mean more to me than a moment."

He stood up and hugged her. "Look I gotta go. It's getting late and I have to get up in the morning. I'll call you tomorrow. And make sure you put your flowers in some water," he said as he left.

Marley laid on the couch feeling restless. She was unsure about what just happened. She figured a little sleep would take her agony away. However, she awoke the next day feeling the same. Something just wasn't right about the night before and it brought tears to her eyes each time she thought about it.

"Felicia, I don't understand what went wrong. I felt the vibes from him the entire evening we were together and it just seemed like the right thing to do at that moment," she said hysterically.

"So have you talked to him yet?" asked Felicia.

"He said he was going to call me today but I haven't heard from him. Why am I feeling so confused about this whole situation? I wanted to show him I appreciated him. I wanted the night to end happily," she said with tears in her eyes.

"Well girl I hate to see you like this. Look Eric and MJ are having a small party. Why don't you come smoke with us and relax your mind. I promise you will feel a lot better after this."

It was evident Marley was trying to convince herself that she was doing the right thing but she failed to realize that Marcus was being gentleman and not the average guy. Marley was afraid of rejection because it meant that she was not allowed to redeem herself. So to avoid it from happening again she decided that she would slowly but surely pull herself away from Marcus. He was a very sincere guy who really would do anything for Marley. She dated Damien for so long and was accustomed to his ways that she wanted every guy to be just like Damien. Now everyone knows that Marley would do anything for Damien and he in return would take anything from Marley. It was that exchange of pleasure and pain that Marley expected from anyone, even her closest friends. She presented herself to the new world as a flourished beautiful rose that would soon wither.

There was no apparent reason in the average persons mind to treat Marcus with a distant attitude. In many ways he was just like Marley, breathing new air but there was one big difference. Marcus was a very sincere person for all the right reasons. It was a natural aura he gave off. However, Miss Marley was beginning to give off a scent that no one was going to enjoy.

The next day she ran into Marcus on campus. He ran up to hug her but was greeted with just a simple "hello". He immediately knew something was wrong with her. It was like with the blink of an eye she changed. She was almost like the American werewolf in his eyes...beautiful, sweet, and humble by day but gruesome, nasty and ruthless by night. Marcus did not like to see Marley this way and he knew this wasn't the Marley he knew from class with class and a beautiful voice to accentuate her persona. Maybe that's it-she was a performer in every aspect of her life. But Marcus was too shallow to figure that out. In his mind she would always be the beautiful Marley he grew to know and right at this very moment she was just going through something-something that would blow away in due time.

Chapter Eight

A new week had come and gone and Felicia was ready to blow the weekend off the map. There was a big concert going down and she won tickets for the official after party. She and Marley received their refunds checks and they were ready to hit the mall.

"Girl I am going to put you on to some club gear today," said Felicia on their way the mall.

"Ok I'm down for a new winter wardrobe. But I promised my parents I would put up some money. Besides my check ain't as big as yours! I need to put my shit on your tab."

"Oh no. That ain't Miss Marley goody too shoes over there with the swearing. Joking girl. Well you can go to the bank and handle that on Monday. I need to hit up the MAC counter and hit up this fly hip hop store for some Roca-Wear."

"So where is this party going to be?"

"Don't worry about the place. Jessica isn't going tonight so it's just me and you."

"Well let's go get our shop on," said Marley as the two entered the mall. It was her first time in a 3 level mall. She couldn't believe her eyes. She had the very same feeling the first day she stepped onto the streets of Chicago. The girls went crazy in the stores. Passing Benjamin's and swiping cards from one store to another. As they walked in the mall Felicia bumped into Troy, someone who she has been waiting to hear from in a while. He has been avoiding her lately and she just couldn't understand why.

"T!" yelled Felicia, "oh you going to walk past me like that, kid." she asked as she approached him rubbing up against him to let anyone know that she was digging him.

"Just chilling. What up Marley Marl," he said as he brushed right past Felicia. Now Felicia could handle a diss from anyone but not in public. She let it ride but she was going to ride him until she found out what was up with him. After he spoke to Marley he told the girls he would holler at them later.

"Wonder what his problem is? You know I haven't spoken to him since that night I went out with Eric."

"Oh yeah he did call but I told him you would call him back."

"You know I was starting to really feel Troy and then all of a sudden he started tripping. I went by his place one day and his roommate was like he ain't here. Girl I looked in the lot and saw his car. So I'm like yeah whatever."

"Y'all haven't sat down and talked about it?" asked Marley. Little did she know she was the reason Troy was acting different.

"You know usually that's who I go hang with and all but since then I just been chilling with Chris, Eric and the other boys. I don't have time for dumb stuff. I'm too smart and fly for all that."

The girls headed back to the apartment to get right for the night. First they stopped by Eric's apartment to have a few drinks and then they went straight to the house to get dolled up. For the first time Marley was able to glitter herself for the night life. And she did. When she stepped in the club that night all of the attention left the ladies in the spot and went straight to the Divas from 4314. The night was just beginning for them and with their VIP passes they walked straight to the VIP with no questions asked. They felt like Hollywood and not to mention they looked like they came straight from Beverly Hills. The girls were having a nice time in the VIP section of the club which overlooked the entire dance floor. There were so many lames from the club sending drinks and flowers to them they were almost toasted by the third drink. As they stood against the rail a familiar face approached Marley.

"Excuse me. Has anyone ever told you you are destined to be a singer?" he whispered in her ear. She turned and smiled at the familiar face.

"How do you know I sing?" she asked with a disturbed look on her face.

"I heard you when you came in the door."

Felicia turned and looked thinking to herself he is so gorgeous but so lame.

"I take it you don't remember me?" he asked Marley.

"You do look familiar but I am not good with names."

"I met you at your fall concert. Me and my partner came out to hear you sing. I'm Dre," he said as he extended a drink to Marley and Felicia.

"Oh ok. I remember. So what are you doing out here."

"Today is my boy's birthday so we decided to have his party at the official concert after party. If you ladies aren't occupied I can show y'all to the real VIP section."

"Sure. Come on Fe Fe. Oh I'm sorry. This is my roomy Felicia. Felicia this is Dre'. He and my choir director work together," said Marley as she introduced the two. She was feeling good and now she felt even better. She could not put her finger on it but she knew tonight was going to be a good night.

They went to the VIP section where Marley met several people from the hottest radio station and not to mention a major star from the concert. Felicia was use to seeing stars. She stayed in the streets of the Manhattan during the summer with her family, where she met just about everyone. Felicia fit right in. It was almost like she was with the squad and Marley was the groupie. Everyone was in chill mode but she was so excited to be in the presence of so many big people. She wanted to take pictures and get autographs and she even tried to sing for one of them. Finally Dre pulled her on the balcony of the VIP section to let her get some fresh air.

"Let me ask you a question Marley," he said to her. "Do you know your purpose for coming to Chicago?"

"I came to go to school and launch my singing career. Why did someone ask about me?"

"Me," he said. She looked at him puzzlingly wondering what Dre would want with her. All she knew about him was he worked with Mr. Jackson from time to time, but what she was about to find out was going to blow her away.

"I am so glad I bumped into you here. I ain't gonna lie girl. You have been on my mind heavily. But you still haven't told me what your purpose is," he said in his sexy voice.

"I just told you Dre. I am here for school and to begin my singing career."

"No let me tell you what your purpose is. You are here to redeem what the world has been waiting for," he said to her as he looked her directly in her eyes. Marley was unsure what he meant but she was ready for whatever he had to offer.

"Do me a favor" he asked her.

"Sure. What can I help you with?"

"Call me tomorrow. Here's my number. Use it. Don't abuse it," he said as he walked away. That totally blew Marley's mind. She had never been approached by a distinguished gentleman before and he was indeed distinguished. She watched him like a hawk as he walked away. He was keen from head to toe with not a mark in sight.

She turned toward the city and it was breathtaking. Marley took in a deep breath and stretched her arms out wide as if she was hugging the city-but unfortunately it did not hug her back.

Chapter Nine

It was Marley's third week in the studio with Dre. She made sure to impress him in any way. Each time she came she was dressed to impress.

"Look Marley. When you come around girl you need to be comfortable. Look at me. T-shirt and ballin' shorts. We chill 'round here but at the same time we stay focused. Aight."

She shook her head to let him know she understood. The last time Dre and Marley met he asked her to write a song and bring to the next session. She was excited with her first task to accomplish. She stayed up all night and day working on her mission. She even missed a study group erasing and writing. Marley enjoyed Dre's company and she learned a lot from him within that short period of time.

"You know what Dre. I'm hot. Can I run home and change clothes?"

"What? Girl we are in the middle of recording this track for you and you want to leave to change. Look in that closet and get a T-Shirt out of there. Ain't nobody here but you and me."

After she changed they sat down to take a break. Dre went over some changes with her and helped her add a new verse to her first song. She was excited about the change. Anything that Dre said or did she agreed to it. She felt he knew it all when it came to music. And she was right. He knew a lot about the industry. Dre was from Atlanta Georgia, the music capital of the south, where talent grew everyday. He told Marley about his production company, shared pictures with her and even invited her to his spot later on for some drinks. At first she hesitated but there was some interest sparking between the two that Dre wouldn't touch and Marley didn't know how to pursue.

Marley opened up to Dre in ways she didn't even have to with Damien. See Damien knew Marley for who he wanted her to be, but Dre wanted to get to know Marley on a deeper level. Dre wanted to know Marley for who she could be. He took her mind places she didn't even know existed. He challenged her and when she failed he would ask her "are you going to redeem yourself to the world or are you going to let the world redeem you?" She didn't understand what he meant but she soon would see her world unfold before her eyes.

Marley's acquaintances began noticing the change in her. She was actually focused; just not on the right things. She was so focused on her singing career that she forgot the reason she was there-school. While sitting in her apartment one day she got a call from her mother.

"Marley. How are you baby?" her mother asked excited to hear her daughter's voice.

"Hey Ma. I'm just sitting here writing," she said with an uninterested tone.

"Am I disturbing you? Tell mama whatcha writing about?"

"Oh I'm just writing a song for a community concert we are having. Me and this other girl are soloist so Mr. Jackson picked us."

"Oh that's nice of him to pick you. What's the song about?" her mother asked.

"Oh it's about family. See we have to perform because it's family weekend in a month. All the high school kids that applied to the school will be here that weekend. It's something new they started this year."

"Oh. Well I was just checking on ya. How are your classes going?" Her mother could tell Marley was focused on something but she was worried about Marley since her grandmother passed. She knew Marley took it hard and even suggested that Marley take the rest of the semester off but that was not a choice for Marley. She had dreams and being home would not help her achieve them.

"So you'll be home for Christmas break right?"

"Actually mom I got a part time job up here so I'll probably stay here and come home for a few days."

"I hope it ain't no boys down there that got your mind twisted every which way." Her mother said jokingly. But Marley was very defensive with her answer.

"Where did that come from? I just told you that I have a job. Gosh ma!" She did not want her parents to know that she has been in a studio recording and out partying with the best of Chicago. They would quickly send for her and she never wanted to give her parents the impression that she would mess up in school. They trusted Marley and that is one of the only reasons they allowed her to go away to school. They knew Marley wanted to be a singer but she advised her parents she was majoring in Education to teach music. She knew how to psyche her parents up and tell them what they wanted to hear. That's how she got her way all her life. There were times when Marley would slip but with the blink of an eye she was right back in place and her parents would never know that she even moved one inch. Instead of them staying on her she stayed on top of their game ahead of the game. That girl had so many tricks up her sleeve even the joker couldn't out do her.

"Well mama's going to let you get back to your song for the concert. You make sure you take some pictures and send them home. We miss you Marley and I know you are making us proud."

"Alright Ma. Tell Jamie and dad I said I love them," she said as she hung up the phone.

She was excited about her song and this time Dre didn't even ask her to write one. It was 11 in the evening and she just couldn't sit still. Marley picked up the phone to call Dre but he didn't answer. It was kind of shocking to her because anytime she called him he picked up the phone. She thought to herself maybe he's busy at this moment. She could not fathom the thought that Dre was not responding to her call. She decided to call him again.

"Hey Dre this Marley. I was just calling to see what's up with you and check on you. Call me back," she said to his voicemail. She turned off the lights and sat in the dark until she fell asleep.

"Marley Sheppard!" yelled Felicia "someone is on the phone for you!"

"Hello," she said in her good morning voice

"Why didn't you pick up the phone when I called you last night? Didn't you tell me to call you back when I got your message?"

"Who is this?" asked Marley not recognizing the voice on the other end of the phone. "Hello?" she said as the person hung up the phone. She rolled over and went back to sleep not even looking on the caller id to see who just called for her.

Later on that day she went on campus to study for her biology test. She met her lab partner at the library as they promised each other they would get a quick study session in.

"Hey Destiny what's up girl?" she asked her lab partner.

"Girl I am tired. I didn't get off of work until 5am this morning. We need to hurry this up. I have to catch some sleep before 11 tonight," said Destiny. She was the same lab partner that cursed Marley out for calling her about missing class. Destiny actually didn't mean any harm by what she said to Marley that day on the phone. She knew Marley was a freshman just trying to help. Destiny even apologized to Marley one day after class. From then on they studied together and if one missed class the other shared notes and assignments.

"Destiny let me ask you a question. Girl where do you shop and get your hair done? You are always looking fly."

"At the mall and my home girl on campus does my hair, but between me and you it ain't mine."

They both laughed hysterically forgetting they were in the library. Marley and Destiny talked for a long time not once touching on the subject of biology. They shared secrets like they were best friends.

"Where do you work so that you are always tired and missing class? Girl I get worried about you sometimes." asked Marley.

"Honestly, between me and You, I'm a dancer at Club Chase. I mean its easy money and I don't do much but shake my ass like I'm at a club."

"Ok let me ask this. Are you making this your profession or something to get by while you are in school?"

"To me it ain't nothing wrong with what I do and how I do it. I like the finer things in life just like stars. Marley I don't do this to get me through school. School is something for me to fall back on. My major is business because I want to open up several kinds of businesses. I'm an entertainer just like the people you see on TV. I just purchased my first car last year and it wasn't some piece of junk to get me around. I bought what I liked-a Benz."

"Wow. I don't know if I could do that. I mean I'm still self-conscious about my body at times."

"Please; that's what they all say," said Destiny as she picked up her things to leave "girl we didn't even study. But I'm sure we'll pass anyway. Just wink at professor and you got an A."

Chapter Ten

When Marley got back to her room she had two messages for her. Both were from Dre. She picked up the phone and called him immediately. She couldn't believe she missed his calls and she knew that he would have something to say. He always told her to call him whenever she left her apartment so that he would know she was preoccupied and anytime she returned she was to call him. He wasn't keeping tabs on her. He was just making sure he would not set up anything knowing she wasn't home. Marley called Dre back to let him know that she was studying. He told her to meet him at her schools gate so they could go to the studio. She packed her bags knowing that if they were at the studio all night she wasn't going to return home that evening.

Marley met Dre at their usual spot. As she got in the car he asked her "what did you tell your girls?"

"What do you mean what did I tell them? I didn't tell them anything," she said with a little jazzitude in her voice.

"Ok," he said as he looked at her with a disappointed look.

Tonight they didn't go to the studio. In fact they went outside of the city. The ride was filled with silence the entire way. Marley fell asleep and when she woke up they were in Atlanta Georgia. They pulled up at a building that looked like a hotel but it was a high rise. Dre took Marley to his place in Atlanta. She was so amazed to be in a new city similar to Chicago. When Marley walked in his place she could smell Dre written all over the place. His scent was one that distinguished him from the rest of the guys she knew. She looked around the place in awe. Every thing was black and white and it did indeed look like a bachelors pad. He had pictures blown up of him and several stars. Dre had statues of panthers everywhere and his living room opened up and overlooked the city. "This is awesome Dre!" screamed Marley.

"Yeah Yeah. Now tell me what your problem is. I should've left you home with that attitude. You know that anytime you leave campus with me you need to tell your roommates what?"

"What. I know," she said playfully. But Dre wasn't playing. The last thing he needed was for someone to think that something was wrong with Marley. She could tell he was getting mad and right at that moment she straightened up.

"Tell me that you told your roommates something Ma. Why are you acting so stupid? I don't have time to play stupid games. I will take you right back to Chi-town and drop you off with that bag like your ass been out on the streets all night. Did you tell your roommates something?" he asked angrily.

"Yes. I left a note that I was going with the concert choir to New York. Is that ok?" she asked in a little girl's voice.

"Is that how we operate? Hell no that ain't ok. Call your roommate right now from this phone card and ask if one of them got your note." Since she was telling a lie she found that impossible. She called her room and let the phone ring twice and hung up. Dre advised her to call back immediately as he knew she was playing him. She didn't want to call back because she was afraid Felicia would pick up the phone. Today they were supposed to go chill with Eric and the fellas. Felicia and Eric purchased drinks. Marley was supposed to buy the chips, dips and wings but she was over 700 miles away from Chicago. She wouldn't make it in enough time to get a buzz. Marley felt crunched and she didn't know what to do. She broke out the tear bucket.

"Look I didn't leave any note or tell my roommates anything. I was so excited to hear from you that I just packed my bag and left." She cried to Dre.

"Well go get your bag off the couch. We are going back to Chicago," he said as he grabbed his car keys.

"But we drove all the way here only to turn around. Dre I'm sorry. I didn't mean to forget."

"That's the problem. It's always you didn't mean to do this or that. Mean it from now own and I'll accept it. But all this whining Ma I don't have time for that! At least if you mean it I'll know that you are not ready for all this."

"But we are here now. I've never been to Atlanta. I want to stay." She cried grabbing his arm.

"Look the only thing you need to grab right now is your bag. Let's go. I'll pull the car around front," he said as he slammed his door. Marley sat on the floor and cried her eyes out. She couldn't believe that they got all the way down there only to turn around. She also couldn't believe Dre was tripping so hard on her not telling her roommates something and definitely not the truth. What Marley failed to realize is that Dre had a purpose for everything he asked of her. He was not hiding anything; he was a person of order who didn't like to be in the mix of ANYTHING!

Marley thought it was stupid for them to leave after such a long drive but to Dre that was nothing. He made that trip twice a week sometimes with sleep and sometimes without.

See Marley had not yet mastered obedience Dre's way. She didn't understand its importance with Dre. She was playing the wrong person.

"Look I brought you here because I thought you were on something different. How about you forget that we ever made this trip. And when you get back to school just figure up something to tell your roommates. You know that you're good at lying"

"Dre why are you acting like this? I just forgot and I told you the truth, damn."

"Can I ask you something? Why did we meet?"

"To fulfill a purpose in each others lives because if I don't redeem myself to the world then the world will redeem me," she said in a sarcastic way. Dre pulled the car over immediately. Now it was one thing to lie to him but another thing to mock him. Here he was trying to get something meaningful inside Marley's head and she was playing games.

"You know what! Forget it. I ain't got time to play. You want to act stupid then we will see how stupid you look when someone else is in that studio singing a number one hit!" he said as he pulled off. "As a matter of fact don't say another word to me." They drove all the way back to Chicago without uttering one word to each other. Dre played instrumentals and a variety of other music. He was showing her what she would be missing if she continued to act the way she did.

They finally arrived at the front gate, the usual spot and before Marley got out the car she reached to hug Dre and to her surprise he hugged her back. She thought to herself things aren't so bad between us after all. Little did she know things were just as they appeared, maybe even worse.

Chapter Eleven

While walking on campus to class Marley bumped into Marcus. They were not friends but they were also not enemies. Marley kept her distance from him but Marcus remained the same. He still called and even ate lunch with her sometimes. He always said encouraging things to Marley because every time he saw her she seemed focused on something else and he was unsure if it was something bothering her or if she was just focused hard on something. They decided to have lunch in the new Café Lots on campus.

"What have you been up to busy lady?" asked Marcus who was just happy to be around her.

"Just chilling and studying hard. Man I think I failed that History quiz we had last Tuesday."

"Well if you would come to class you probably would have passed. I told you if you were going to be out to let me know and I would stop by with the notes. Girl you can't start slipping now at the end of the semester," he said showing his concern.

"I know right. Things just haven't been the same since my grandmother passed," she said it like she was looking for sympathy. Marley did indeed miss her grandmother but that was really the last person on her mind. She was thinking about Dre especially since she hasn't heard from him in a few days.

"You'll get through it Marley. I know it's hard because it was so sudden but you'll make it. You're strong when you think you're weak," he said to her rubbing her back.

She missed Marcus at times but then she quickly reminds herself that she has to focus on the one who will make her dreams of singing come true-Dre.

"Girl you are beautiful. Man I wish we were in the next lifetime. I would sweep you off your feet," he said with excitement.

"We already tried that Marcus and it didn't work," she said laughingly. Marcus accepted that he and Marley were just "Cool". That was better than not having her in his life at all.

"Look I gotta go. I promised a classmate I would meet with her for our project in 20 minutes. Marley grabbed her stuff and dashed out the door. She was to call Dre in 20 minutes and it took her 20 minutes to get home. Using her track skills she sprinted across the campus in no time.

She made it home just in time to call him.

"Dre. What's up?" she said as she tried to catch her breath.

"Ok. I see you on something different today. What's up for later? You want to come through and put something on today." He asked her. He was a little proud of her and she could hear it in his voice.

"Ok. I'll call you around 9pm. Is that ok?"

"Yeah that's straight. You make sure you handle your business before you meet me at the gate. Aright."

"See you at nine," she said as she hung up the phone. She was so excited and it showed all over her face. She packed her bag, showered, did her hair and make up and picked out 3 hot outfits in case they went out.

Nine o'clock came around and she stood at the gate waiting for him. Unfortunately he did not show up on time. Dre showed up an hour late but Marley did not leave. She wanted to see her Dre so bad that she waited until 10pm and when he pulled up she got in the car with no questions asked as if they set the time for 10. When they got to the studio there were a few of Dre friends there and he introduced Marley to them. She put her bag down and went straight for the booth. They recorded 5 tracks that night and all the guys were feeling her skills. She even tried hip hop rhymes in a few of the songs with upbeats and with the adlibs it made the tracks hotter than hot. Her voice was tired and water would not help. She asked Dre if she could come sit with him and his friends while they smoke and to her surprise, he said yes. The whole evening was rather shocking since Marley never met any of his friends before and anytime he smoked he would tell her to go in another room. Not tonight. It was almost like she was off of some kind of punishment. But it wasn't punishment. It was Dre being easy. He always told her the more she improved the easier things would be between them.

Marley was chilling and feeling good. She was feeling so good she started dancing to the music, a few songs which were hers played on the mix tape. Before Marley knew it she and Dre were in the booth making a mix of their own. She was so gone she didn't even realize the crowd had disappeared and it was only the two of them and the music connection in the air. Marley caressed Dre like the notes caressed the staff on paper. Their bodies twisted and turned and jerked with each beat of the song. Now that's called making music.

Chapter Twelve

Marley and Destiny had a final exam presentation to complete and turn in by Friday. It was the end of the semester and Marley was playing catch up. For a while she had been chasing other things instead of the right things. All the girls were going to stay in Chicago for the winter break and since they were off campus they were not required to leave. As Destiny and Marley were studying Destiny asked Marley a question she would never have thought to hear.

"Marley I need a favor?" asked Destiny.

"What's up De?"

"I have a party to do this weekend for the football players and there are 20 of them and 3 of us. We need one more girl to help us. You don't have to strip. Just wear a sexy outfit and dance. You can make a quick $350 for 3 hours."

"Girl I don't know. I am too ashamed to show my body. You see my little roll here and there. And anyways I can't dance."

"Come on Marley. Please do me this one favor. Girl you look fine. You'll be just fine. I mean they are just football players. I've had my share of stars. That's when you need to worry about what you look like. This one time please."

"Ok, but I have to make sure I don't have any plans. You know my boy might come through and scoop me up for the weekend," she said excitingly when she spoke of this mysterious man.

She went home and called Dre to make sure they didn't have any plans for this weekend. It's not like he would have told her 4 days earlier. She knows that he is a spur of the moment person and hardly does any planning for pleasure. She reminisced on the day she and Dre "made love" in the booth. It was magical. She couldn't believe it herself. She vowed after that night to give her all and all to him. He was the most important person in her life right now.

"Ma you know I don't plan several days ahead of time. Not for the studio. Why what's up?" he asked her.

"Let me ask you a question. I feel comfortable enough to ask you this. Do you think it would be hoeish of me to dance at a party? I mean someone asked me but I didn't make any promise yet," she said lying to him. She already had her mind made up. She just wanted to hear what he had to say about a female dancing for some guys.

"What you want me to say. That's exactly what it is-dancing. Do your thang Ma. Are you making any money from it?" he asked surprisingly.

"What. You mean that ain't unladylike to you?" She asked surprised at his question.

"Look Marley. You are beautiful. You are talented. And you are smart. Use your mind, body and soul to get you where ever you want to be. I can't knock your hustle. Please I know plenty of girls who strip and dance but they are no where near as smart as you. What you thought I was going to say no?" he laughed.

"I ain't going to do it. I was just asking." she said. She couldn't believe what she just heard. Dre was joking her to dance half naked in front a group of guys.

She decided not to do it now. The fact that he joked about her dancing wasn't clear to her. Marley expected him to tell her no or tell her she was out of character. She was confused as to why he didn't say no so she decided to ask him.

"Why are you telling me to dance or as you said do your thang Ma?" asked Marley. She wanted to know for certain why he would allow her to do something society found so degrading.

"I'm actually not for all of that but the fact that you could come to me and ask me about it let's me know that you are growing. See I expected you to go behind my back and do something and then call me like nothing ever happened. Ma, you know I appreciate that. I really do," he said.

That was all she needed to hear from Dre was how much he appreciated her. She made sure that she was to show him too how much she appreciated him. At this point Marley said to herself she was going to do the party and surprise Dre with something as soon as the party was over.

Saturday came and all day Marley was very jittery. She and Felicia even argued over something interesting that Felicia found out.

"Marley, can I ask you a question?" said Felicia.

"What's up Fe Fe.?"

"Actually I got two questions. The first question is what's going on with you? You're starting to act a little different." asked Felicia with concern.

"I'm cool. Just trying to stay focused. Sometimes I just want to be alone. You're staying here during the break right?"

"Yeah. Ok. Look I'm not mad. I just need you to be honest with me, the night I went out with Eric did you tell Troy that I was out was out with Eric?"

"No. I said exactly what you told me to say," said Marley. She remembered telling Troy about Eric because she did not even know that Felicia liked Troy until they went to the mall that Saturday.

"Ok. Well, Troy said word for word what you told him. And Marley right now at this point it's the principal. You sat there in the mall and that was when you could have brought it up. If you did not know that we liked each other so what. I told you to say a certain thing and you did as you felt. You are mad cool girl and I dig you as a friend, sister, roommate and all, but you have habits and ways that you covered when you first moved here. That innocent mess I saw right through it. So do you but don't mess me over in the process."

"Felicia. I told him what you told me to tell him. I'll call Troy myself." screamed Marley.

"Whoa. To lie to me is one thing but to play me stupid means that you don't even care. Know what I'm saying. Just drop it. Remember you don't have to lie to protect yourself or because you think that I am going to do something back to you. I ain't like you. I don't push my friends to the side or lie to people. You need to slow down girl. I don't know what is really going on with you but whatever it is please just keep it real with me," said Felicia as she slammed Marley's bedroom door. Whatever Marley thought to herself. She had a party to get ready for. She couldn't believe that Felicia was tripping over something old and to Marley she shouldn't have been sneaking around on Troy anyway. He was such a nice guy.

It was more than just Felicia versus Troy. She trusted Marley as a friend to do as she asked of her; to protect her even if she was doing the unthinkable. Marley just couldn't understand the principle of what Felicia just said. She really didn't care because to her that was old news. She had a party to attend and she was going to make it one of the best nights of her life.

Marley called Destiny and they met at a guy's house off campus. Everyone was talking about this party all week. The football team had a successful season and this was their first Saturday off. The party was packed when Marley and Destiny came out. Marley looked like a playboy bunny dressed in all black lingerie she picked up from Victoria Secrets, but Marley begin to panic. She saw so many familiar faces there and she felt embarrassed. Destiny called her in the back room and gave her a cigarette and a drink to make her calm down. In deed she did. After about 30 minutes she begin twisting and turning like she was a professional dancer. Rhythm wasn't her thing in the past but that night it was her best friend. Her body swayed left right front back up and down. And she had all the attention. No one had ever seen this side of Marley. Even Marley didn't know that she had it in her. As she moved her body in front of a few football players they tossed out big money and she picked up every last dollar not knowing her soul was the price. She was in another world after she regained her high. She was so gone she didn't realize that she was dancing for Marcus and his roommate, who was also a football player.

"Ay Marcus. Ain't that the chick you used to mess with? The one who tried to play you at the stop sign that day. Oo wee! I didn't know she had all that under those clothes," he said with excitement. Marcus couldn't believe his eyes. Marley was so gone she didn't even recognize him. He stood there in disbelief. He felt sorry for the person she had become and the beautiful person she left behind. The more he stared at her the angrier he became. He pulled Marley to the side and she quickly snapped on him not realizing who he was.

"Get off me muthafu...Marcus. What are you doing here?" she asked with her words slurring.

"The sober Marley would have never cursed. In fact the sober Marley would have never been here," said Marcus disappointingly.

"Just trying to make a little extra cash and have fun. It's just clean fun. I ain't sleeping with no one. And besides my boy said it's all right with him," she said happily telling herself she was doing this because of Dre's approval.

"Any man that let's his girl do this ain't worth the dollar you just made. You should be ashamed of yourself."

"You know what Marcus it would've never worked with us because you are so close-minded!" she yelled at him and walked away. He didn't mean to make her upset but it made Marcus upset to see Marley like this. He pulled out his wallet and gave Marley 150 dollars. His last 150 dollars.

"If this helps you get out of here faster here. Take this and please go home," he said as he put the money in her hand. He was fighting a battle on both sides that was nearly over but he wouldn't give up. He couldn't give up on the girl he had feelings for, even if she didn't love him back.

Chapter Thirteen

"Marley where are you" asked Dre. He was upset that Marley was late for the meeting with Chi's-Own. They were supposed to be recording a track in the studio that day with Marley.

Not only was she 30 minutes late but she also came to the studio looking like she was going to the club. "Man she's fine!" yelled one of the guys in the group. They watched Marley prance in her black stiletto heels with her tube top dress from the time she got in the door until the time she left their presence to have a talk with Dre.

"Marley how many times do I have to tell you to come here comfortable and stop looking like you are about to go out? Now go in the back and put on that t-shirt and those shorts. And I'm gonna get at you later for being late. I don't like that at all," said Dre. She nodded her head and did as told. There was something about Dre that made Marley obey his every word. He tells her that he knew she was destined to be a star from the first time he heard her on stage and he meant that.

Marley stepped in the booth and blew the guys away. She added and subtracted lyrics from the hook that would add flavor to the track they recorded. She was a genius with the words and with her voice. The two together would take Marley to the top as long as she stayed focused. The guys liked working with Marley and once the song was recorded, Dre called Studio O to set up a performance.

"Everyone needs to be back in the studio tomorrow at 5pm. Not 5:01. The performance will be next Friday night. I'll gather up the street team to put the word on the street. It's on! Hope y'all ready," said Dre as he shut the door behind the guys.

"Dre that might be a problem because I promised Felicia she and I would go to the mall tomorrow to shop."

"So when are you going to learn how to prioritize. You don't see anyone else coming at me saying they had a shopping spree scheduled so they can't come. I swear sometimes Baby Girl you ain't as hungry as you say you are."

"Dre it's not even like that. I promised Felicia that I would go shopping with her this time since I have been pushing back our shopping time."

"And I get sick of telling you to be on time. Do you know how that makes me look in front of people? Here I am telling people you are fly and your voice is so hot it's scary and you come 30 minutes late or whenever you feel like it."

"I don't know who is going to be here so I have to make sure that I look right," said Marley in defense of herself.

"Marley you know what, don't even worry about it. If you feel that shopping and being late is better than recording a number one hit then go ahead. Call me when you get serious. I get sick of telling you the same lines over and over. Just leave. I'm about to lock up."

"But Dre" she cried as he shut the door. This wasn't their first falling out. In fact it happened more that she could remember. For some apparent reason Marley still had not mastered the art of obedience in the eyes of Dre. She thought as long as she recorded a hot song then she could do what ever she wanted. She gave him 100% of her voice but not much of herself and that is what created the distance between them.

She headed home to call Dre but there was one thing that boggled her mind. She did not know how to tell Felicia that she would either have to go shopping the next day or early. She had plans with Dre at 5 and she couldn't miss this but at the same time she couldn't push her friend off another day. Marley decided to ask Felicia if they could go early and that way she could be back in time to meet Dre at 5.

Unfortunately Felicia couldn't go early that day or the next day. For some reason Marley didn't care. Dre was the main person she had to impress. However, she failed to realize impressing him was not the key. Letting him take total lead of her was the key to their success. Marley was learning that slowly but surely but how long would it take her to master her weakness-obedience.

She was on time and ready to start recording the track with the group. They were already a hot group locally who were trying to get their hits recognized nationally and Dre felt with Marley on the hook they all would be on their way to the top. The group along with Marley put out a hot track and Dre had the equipment in his studio to print a disc and send it on its way. He even had a surprise for them that night. They would be opening up for a major artist at the spring fling concert held each year on campus. They all were excited especially Marley. She began visioning herself on stage with the crowd going wild.

"Dre are you serious!" she screamed.

"Now this is in less than two months so I say the fellas lay two tracks and Marley you lay two tracks and then you all do one together. I am going to see if we can perform one song each and then one song together. I know in order to do that we are going to have to run the songs together to make it less than 10 minutes because that's all we have." They were real excited. Marley could not believe she would be performing as an opening act for the artist next week.

She ran up to Dre and gave him big never let me go hug. Marley was ready to see herself blossom but her ways would soon catch up with when she least expects it.

She ran home to tell her roommates about the news regarding the concert. She was so excited about the performance. She tried calling Damien but there was no answer or a voicemail option. Marley couldn't sit still and she moved around so much to bring attention to herself. It was like she yearned for others to show concern about her but when it came to others she lacked the characteristic of caring. Now it wasn't that she didn't care about anyone. She was a very sincere person at heart. It's just she has allowed habits that can't be broken to enter her world by living for the moment.

She went back out to get some fresh air and she decided to walk to Blockbuster since it was just down the block. As she was going in Blockbuster she passed Marcus. He gave her a sympathetic look and she told him he didn't have to feel sorry for her. It was only fun. See Marley didn't know how to let go of things either. She was the type to carry it on until it breaks her back.

Marcus did not mention anything regarding the party. He was only approaching her to speak and see how she was doing. As soon as he heard Marley say what she said to him he quickly turned and went the opposite way. When Marley is serious she wants everyone to be serious with her and when she is in joyful mood she wants everyone to be excited with her. However, it didn't work like that for everyone. That was another big problem of Marley's. She was an emotional rollercoaster all the time.

It's written all over her face that she is not a consistent person even though she could be. Marley's struggle did not develop overnight. These are habits she brought with her to Chicago. She had a problem with being left alone for long periods of time but at the same time she enjoyed a few hours to herself from time to time. Marley didn't understand that because she was feeling a certain way everyone didn't have to feel the same exact way. Her happiness came from various outlets. She tried for so long to hold up to her words, especially for Damien. She knew that she couldn't let him down. However, the way things go with Marley you may never know what to expect from her. She is good at acting and even she knows that she is. That's why she is able to maneuver her way through her trials and tribulations. Like Mama Sheppard told her "don't let nobody hold you back".

Marley met up with Dre later on that evening for dinner and they enjoyed each others company. Marley was catching feelings for Dre hard and he even admitted that he was starting to feel Marley on another level, but they had to stay focused on their purpose. Marley appreciated the talks she and Dre had. She knew that he was going to point her in the right direction. Marley spent the night with Dre and the entire evening they dedicated it getting to know who Marley D really was and what she really wanted.

Meanwhile Felicia was waiting for Marley the next morning since she rescheduled the shopping spree. She waited for 3 hours and Marley didn't even show or call. Felicia was beginning to worry even though she knew Marley was somewhere on campus. She decided to go alone.

Felicia was beginning to see another side of Marley that she questioned. Marley came to Chicago with a very positive outgoing attitude and when she first arrived you could tell she was really interested in college life. However, the more Marley hung out the less you were able to see if the real version of Marley she created when first arrive for school even existed. She wasn't a master of her own art. She was too busy trying to cover her tracks or master someone else's that she lost herself in the entire process of coming to school to get an education. It was going to be hard to deal with her if she continued down the road she was currently traveling. Her deceitful, irresponsible ways were soon to catch up with her.

Chapter Fourteen

Marley met up with Dre to go over the song she wanted to use for the concert. She felt good about the song she wrote. However, Dre had something else in mind. He wanted a song that would not clash with what the group was performing. It made Marley upset but she would not show Dre her anger because she knew it would spark a disagreement. She has been following his lead for a while but now she just wanted to write a song that she felt would be a number one hit for her.

Marley brought a lot of attention to herself and all of it wasn't good attention. She and Destiny were becoming close friends and Marley even found herself doing private parties with Destiny and she gave herself the name Fantasy. It was quick money for her and she promised herself she would not get too caught up in it. No one knew but her and Destiny. Marley was not flourishing as the beautiful rose she hoped to soon become. Instead she was more like a withered flower at this point.

There was not a day that went by where something didn't bother Marley. She didn't like being under pressure and making decisions was not her specialty. Marley was not a leader in any shape, form, or fashion. She needed guidance in every aspect of her life. And Dre provided that for her. She knew that without Dre she would not have been able to do this on her own. In a sense she was using Dre because her whole purpose was to get a song on the radio for Damien. Now of course she loved Dre but her heart was with Damien.

Things were not going so smooth back at 4314. There was a lot of tension in the air. Felicia was not talking to Marley or Jessica and Jessica wasn't talking to Marley. With three women, under one roof there was no way there was not going to be another screaming match. Felicia was mad at both Jessica and Marley because they both told Troy the same thing about her and Eric. Marley was getting tired of hearing Felicia cry the same old song about Troy and Jessica's problem was because Marley came in late or didn't leave her messages of her where-abouts. Marley thought to herself "This is the same chick who told me she would curse me out too for trying to keep tabs on everyone." Marley liked Jessica but she was a little too nit picky for Marley. She felt she and Felicia were good friends but Felicia was acting distant. She was not being snobby about not talking to Marley or Jessica. As a matter of fact she always spoke to them and carried on small talk but as far as trusting them, especially Marley, that was out the window.

Marley started getting bad vibes about the way things were going in her apartment. She went to the residential advisor on campus to check out the campus housing and she even picked up some apartment guides along her way. Trying to keep them concealed when she returned to the apartment, she ended up dropping every thing. Climbing up the last flight of stairs she bumped into Felicia who was on her way out. Felicia didn't say one word; not even excuse me. To add insult to injury, she didn't even offer to help Marley pick up her things.

As Felicia spitefully stepped over Marley she noticed the apartment guide lying on the floor. And for Marley to not even mention it to Felicia or Jessica, Felicia felt very disrespected, especially when they accrue small bills like electricity, cable, and gas. Felicia turned around when she got outside the build-ing. It really bothered her that Marley was considering moving out. She wanted some answers regarding the many questions that ran through her mind.

"Marley can we vibe for a minute." asked Felicia.

"What's up?"

"I see you have your apartment guides around. Are you planning to leave here soon?" asked Felicia in her Philly girl stance.

"I just want to do something different. And honestly I feel like people don't want me around so why not. You have been acting real shady towards me lately and I know why but I still consider you to be my girl through thick and thin," said Marley.

"Ok I can accept that coming from you. I just hope that whatever keeps you focused on what you are doing now doesn't ruin your life," said Felicia as she walked out the door. She and Marley have their little quarrels from time to time but some how they always end up laughing about it later.

Marley met up with Dre that evening to discuss some of her plans. She mentioned that she wanted to move on campus or either in her own apartment and that's when Dre told her she could stay with him until she figured out what she wanted to do. Marley was surprised that he even asked her especially since they agree to disagree on a weekly basis. Spring Break was around the corner and so was the big concert.

Dre had Chi's Own and Marley in the studio doing a test performance every day up until the concert day. Marley had already made plans for spring break. She, Veronica, Destiny and Felicia were going to Daytona Beach. They had their bags packed early because their plane was leaving early that morning of the concert. Now Marley really had something large on her plate to juggle. How was she going to perform and be in Daytona at the same time? She had to think of something quick because time was not on her side. She decided to pass up the concert and go to Daytona, a place she has never been. She felt she deserved a break. Lately all she had been doing was recording, recording and more recording. Marley didn't see any harm in going away for her spring break instead of performing at the concert. She felt that if Dre gave her a shot and helped her then anyone can. She had been avoiding her friends on a regular basis to record in the studio or hang out with Dre.

Even though Marley felt that she deserved a break from the studio she failed to realize that if she did not show up it will affect her future as well as the credibility of Dre. Not to mention that Chi's Own and Marley worked on a track together. That means that if she doesn't show up Chi's Own will not be able to perform the last song with everyone on it. It was going to be a disaster but Marley didn't see it that way. She felt the show would go on with or without her.

On the day of the concert the girls were boarding their plane and Marley was flying in the friendly skies forgetting all her troubles. She still hadn't thought of a good excuse as to why she couldn't make it to the concert. "I had to go home for a family emergency" she kept repeating in her head but she was afraid to use that one. Lord knows what she would do if something really happened to someone in her family but in desperate situations that seemed like the only excuse she could give Dre. As a matter of fact, the entire time she was in Daytona she didn't call Dre.

Chapter Fifteen

"This trip is going to be exciting" Marley thought to herself while on the plane. The entire flight she and Destiny discussed all the possible mischievous flings they could get into during Spring Break. For Destiny this was just another week off from school but for Marley this was a new place with new adventures. Once they arrived at their hotel, Veronica and Felicia headed straight for their rooms to rest. They were exhausted from loading and unloading and stopping and going through so many different airports.

"I can't hang right now," said Felicia. "I don't feel too good after that last take off."

"Me neither," said Veronica. She lived downstairs from the girls. They always bumped into Veronica at one of their many club rendezvous. She was a junior in college and each spring break her parents allowed her to take 3 of her friends to any one of their resorts. This year she picked Daytona.

"Veronica this room is so nice" yelled Marley forgetting the girls were trying to rest.

"Let's go Marley. I see some things on the beach I want to try," said Destiny as she looked over the balcony at the large spring break crowd. The girls changed into their swim wear and headed straight for the sun and waves.

The atmosphere was full of music from hip hop to rock. There were girls in bikinis screaming, guys in shorts surfing, girls tanning and guys staring. Oh yeah the scent in the air yelled Spring Break. For some reason as excited as she seemed, Marley wasn't in touch with the crowd.

"I don't know about you Destiny but I ain't feeling these people too much. They are doing their own thing, ya know."

"Just chill out for a minute. Believe me it gets better during the night. I just like coming to the beach to walk and listen to the different music," said Destiny. She wasn't so into the club scene for spring break since she has seen enough of it back in Chicago. For her this was supposed to be relaxing during the day and whatever the night decided to bring she was sure to take it. See, Marley envisioned spring break just as she saw it on TV-wild and fun with surprises and sleepless nights. She thought the minute she stepped off the plane it would be party city. It even surprised her that Felicia was in the room sleep. She knew for sure the Felicia would have been the first one making plans for the day and the night.

The girls decided to grab something for lunch at one of the spots on the beach. The arrived at a spot where a large crowd gathered to listen to a band. For the past couple of months Destiny and Marley were hanging strong from the parties they did together to just going to pick up lunch. You would not see one without the other. People were starting to believe Marley was Destiny's roommate. However, her evening time was juggled between dancing and singing.

Marley was beginning to view her part time job as something that would take her places she could only imagine in her dreams. That was the same feeling she use to have for singing. The more money she made the less attention she paid to her purpose and true passion. Now when it came to going to the studio she never missed a session and she still did what was expected of her by Dre. There was a lot that she was hiding from him but everything that was hidden would soon come to the surface. Right at that very moment Marley was supposed to be on stage performing and singing her heart out. The concert was going to put Marley in a position to receive everything she asked and yearned for but instead the beach took her concentration momentarily.

"Marley what do you want to drink?" asked Destiny as she looked at the menu trying to decide what to have for lunch.

"Give me a strawberry daiquiri," she said. It was never too early for Marley to sip on anything especially since it was spring break.

"Girl do you see what I see?" asked Marley pointing to some guys that were eying her for the longest. "I'll invite them up!"

"Whoa! I am sure we'll meet plenty of those while we are here. Let's just chill for now" exclaimed Destiny as she wanted Marley's company.

"Girl loosen up. We are here to have fun!" said Marley as she waved to the guys to come up. "We are about to get a free meal so act like you are interested," she said as they both laughed.

The guys came to the table and ordered appetizers and more alcohol. After they socialized at the table they danced and drunk more and more. Marley began to feel dizzy with the mixture of heat and the large crowd.

"De, I am too tipsy to walk. Hold up. Please let me sit down" asked Marley as she fanned herself from the heat wobbling from side to side to keep her balance.

Destiny splashed water on her and pulled her all the way back to the room where Felicia and Veronica were up chatting from their nap.

"What! She's plastered already!" yelled Felicia "she is the only chick I know who can't hold her liquor." She told the girls about their first club incident and many there after and everyone laughed, even Marley. She and Felicia had their ups and downs but Felicia said she would always be cool with Marley. Felicia wasn't a wishy washy girl. She remained the same person Marley met at the beginning of the school year.

The girls made plans to go club hopping that night but now Marley wasn't feeling so well from all the drinks she had earlier. As she got up from the couch she said to the girls, "I think that boy Chad slipped me a Mickey."

"Girl please you've had worse." laughed Felicia as they all made jokes at Marley. She decided to stay in that night. The girls got dressed and Marley fell asleep on the couch.

Felicia, Veronica and Destiny were up and down the boulevard that night. By the time they were heading to the third club Destiny said she was tired and went back to the room.

When she arrived back in the room she noticed Marley on the balcony smoking a cigarette and enjoying the breeze.

"Where's everybody?" asked Marley as she entered in the room.

"Girl my feet are killing so I decided to put them to rest. Let's go get in the Jacuzzi downstairs."

They put on their swim suits and went downstairs to enjoy the relaxing environment. The girls were both relaxing while Marley talked to Destiny about her feelings for Dre. She laid her head back on the wall of the Jacuzzi thinking how things would be had she stayed in Chicago to do the concert but those thoughts were quickly interrupted by Destiny.

"Stop thinking about whatever it is so hard. Relax your mind. It'll smooth over," said Destiny.

"Maybe. Maybe not" sighed Marley as she tried to relax. She closed her eyes and drifted back to Chicago dreaming of herself singing on the stage doing what she loved the most. Her deep thoughts were interrupted by Destiny stroking her hair and Marley didn't mind. She just laid back and closed her eyes tighter. They both sat in the Jacuzzi and relaxed while Destiny stroked her friend's problems away.

The girls headed back to the room where they found a note from Veronica and Felicia stating they bumped into some guys from campus so they would be home with the rising of the sun. Marley hopped in the shower to get ready for bed while Destiny did the same.

In the room they laid wrapped in their towels on their beds staring at the ceiling searching for words.

"Destiny do you ever get tired of dancing. I know I do sometimes," said Marley.

"Sometimes I do. Other times I don't. It depends on how I feel at that exact moment. I like private parties better because you never see the same faces like you would in a club"

"True. That last party was ok. The thing that keeps me going is the money girl. I've never made that much money to spend on myself."

"Yeah and it's even worth all the extra stuff. My sister is always telling me I'm too beautiful to let the world enjoy me for a moment."

"You ever think she's right. I mean honestly beauty means a lot to me now. I love how much attention and compliments I get now."

"Marley I've always thought you were beautiful. From the first time I saw you I knew your beauty would take control of the world. Now look where it's gotten you," said Destiny as she moved out of her bed closer to Marley and stared in her eyes. She felt very close to Marley in ways no one would understand.

Marley looked back at Destiny and whispered in her ear "you are beautiful too". In the midst of compliments Marley felt a feeling she has never felt before-guilty pleasure. At that moment tears begin to roll down her eyes and her new found friend leaned forward and kissed her ever so softly. Lost in ecstasy the forbidden fruit brought comfort to Marley's lonely heart that no one could decipher.

While that connection sparked in a new place back in Chicago Dre put to rest the connection Marley was supposed have with the world. As she explored her Destiny passionately, Chicago ripped her off the streets. Every poster of Marley and Chi's Own was shredded and it left a mark on Dre that no one would ever forget. Marley missing the show started a domino effect in his world. With her not showing up it threw the entire show off schedule not to mention all the money, time and effort he spent on his new found star. Dre was furious and as Marley sparked a new fire he put out the flames that would allow her to burn the world with her style and her voice. The fire that she was supposed to bring would bring so much heat to the industry-just like the burning passion she was making at that exact moment.

Veronica and Felicia came back from their late night rendezvous. The girls had a good time with their friends from campus. They were too tired to even notice Marley and Destiny had their own late night rendezvous.

For the rest of the trip all the girls had a blast. They left a mark on the beach that no one would forget. Marley tried surfing, Destiny did a wet tee contest, Felicia entered a dance contest and Veronica, well just say girls gone wild.

Chapter Sixteen

When Marley got back to Chicago she continued to think of excuses she could tell Dre. She was too nervous to pick up the phone to call him but she knew she needed to talk to him. Dialing Dre's number was the most difficult thing for Marley to do. She quickly hung up the phone and decided to call him later. Felicia came in the room to say good night. She was tired ready to take a break from her Spring Break.

"How did the conversation go with your friend?" asked Felicia.

"Oh everything is cool. I'm about to go to bed now," said Marley hoping that everything really was cool but realizing that it wasn't. Marley looked around the dark room trying to fall asleep to wake up from what she wanted to be a dream. She tossed and turned all night thinking of Dre. The phone rung and she quickly picked up only to find out it wasn't the person she was thinking of.

"You alright Marley?" asked Destiny. She called to check on her friend after their long spring break.

"Look I'm sleepy Destiny. Can I call you tomorrow?" she asked. Marley didn't feel up to Destiny at that moment and she really didn't want to bring the fling from Daytona. Marley was a moment person. For Marley what happened in a moment stayed in that moment and this was no exception.

"Alright girl. Well call me tomorrow. Maybe we can do lunch or go shopping," said Destiny as she hung up the phone. Marley listened to the dial tone for several seconds and dialed her true destiny.

The phone rung a few times and someone picked up the phone but didn't say anything.

"Dre it's me Marley. Hello?" she said repeatedly but still no answer from the other end of the phone. She then heard a dial tone and dialed the number again.

"Dre this is Marley. I need to talk to you" she cried repeatedly. "I need you to say something to me!" she screamed and heard a dial tone again. It crushed Marley that he wouldn't talk to her. The dead silence on the phone hurt more than any lecture Dre gave her in the past. She would rather Dre yell at her than to say nothing at all.

For the next couple of days Marley tried to reach Dre but she was unsuccessful. She heard not a single word from him. She sat in her room for a whole week staring at the poster of her on the wall. It was the poster to promote her for the concert. She looked beautiful on the picture. Never once had she imagined her beauty the way it was painted on the picture. Never once did she imagine she would even be on a poster.

Marley woke up and decided to take a walk in the middle of the night. The air was crisp and warm enough for a walk alone. As she walked she stared at the ground and carefully watched her steps as if she was walking on the edge. Every now and then she would look up to see where she was going. Her eyes followed her feet instead of her carefully watching what was in her view. That's what got Marley to where she ended up following the wrong dreams and abandoning her own.

As she approached the campus she noticed for the first time its serene beauty. The campus was well-lit with tall buildings staggered on each corner. There were groups of people on the lawn, on the stairs of buildings and walking the campus. It was like a small city being consumed by a larger city. Her freshman year flew by her so fast and it dawned on her that she didn't enjoy like most first year students. She wasn't involved with campus activities. She didn't have any friends on campus and barely recognized her classmates from her classes in the second semester. While sitting on the stoop of the library she saw Marcus and he saw her. But for the first time he kept walking. Not because he didn't want to talk to her. It was because he didn't recognize her. She wasn't the person he met last semester. Her lifestyle not only changed her way of living it changed her looks, her talk and the way she carried herself. It hurt that Marcus didn't come over to speak to her but it hurt her more that he didn't recognize her.

She immediately left the campus and began walking to find Dre. She knew the way to the studio and she prayed the entire way that Dre would be there.

As Marley walked the sidewalks she saw so many things that reflected the direction her life headed. There were home-less people begging for her help. She walked past a mother crying for her child who had been shot. Two people were engaged in a verbal disagreement over money. A woman asked her if she wanted to buy some jewelry. Across the street from the stop light as she stopped a beautiful woman walked pass her with a fur coat on and fish net tights approaching every car that stopped. She noticed she was lost deep in the city and everything she saw before her eyes frightened her.

Marley stopped at a payphone to call Dre to come and get her.

"Dre please don't hang up. I need your help. I'm lost and I can't find my way to the studio." She cried.

"What do you see around you?" he asked.

"I'm over by the club I met you at. There is a check cashing place on the corner. I can't see the street sign from here."

"Oh. I know where you are. So what do you want me to do?" he asked nonchalantly.

"Please come get me. I need to talk to you as soon as possible."

"Ok. I'll hear you out. Give me about 20 minutes to close up shop," he said as he hung up the phone. Marley turned around facing the club where she met her destiny and on the light pole in her face was a ripped poster of her for the concert. Just like the poster her life was shredded. She waited for an hour before she tried to call Dre back but only got his voicemail. She was alone with no direction and no one to guide her. She broke down in tears as she began heading in the direction toward campus.

As she walked she felt as if she was being followed and in deed she was. Marley walked faster and the foot steps be-hind her picked up the pace. She approached a busy intersec-tion and too afraid to stop she stepped on the busy street only to see her life flash before her eyes.

"Watch out lady!" yelled the voice behind her. "I was trying to catch up with you to give you your keys. You left them on the payphone back there," said the man.

"Oh thank you sir," said Marley almost out of breath.

"You shouldn't be out here alone. Where do you live?" he asked.

"Oh I'm almost home. Thanks again," she said as she hurried across the street. The only thing that replayed in her head was the flashing lights of the cab as she stepped on the busy street. She began crying unstoppably. In her mind she knew Dre was going to come to her rescue and hear her out, but why should he. Why should anyone?

She decided to pay Destiny a visit. It was late but she needed someone to talk to and she knew Destiny would listen.

"Come in girl. What's up?" asked Destiny as she let Marley in.

"I just don't know what went wrong? What is going on with me?" she cried to her friend.

"What do you mean?"

"No one is talking to me. Dre left me hanging in the middle of no where. This guy was chasing me and he said because I left my keys at the payphone. I almost got hit by a car. Marcus didn't even notice me tonight on campus. He was walking with some girls," she said as she cried for comfort and sympathy. However, she didn't get it. See Destiny had been trying to reach Marley for the past week and she avoided her in all ways. Now that she needed comfort she looked to Destiny for it.

"What's been going with you Marley? I mean lately you been screening your calls from me. The other day I saw you at the cafeteria and you tried to avoid me. What's up with that?"

"I didn't see you. And I haven't been home to receive your calls. I need to talk to you about some things and this is what I get?" yelled Marley. She didn't understand why the world was coming down on her or not even coming to her at all. She was mad that everyone made everything her fault and the fact that Destiny didn't offer to comfort her made her more upset.

"I ain't even going to get on that with you. Besides I saw Felicia and she said you've been home all week. You didn't go to any of your classes. I just wanted to make sure you're all right."

Without even thinking about the statement Destiny said Marley yelled, "Look! It ain't anything between me and you. I don't need you trying to hover over me like you are my man. I don't even get down like that! Just let that spring break drama go! I wouldn't be going through this if I wasn't in Daytona with you! "

"First of all I considered you a friend and I wanted to make sure that you were ok. But since you think someone is jocking you how about you jock your yellow self right out my apartment. That's why your world is upside down now! Everything you did and said came right back to you!" yelled Destiny as Marley slammed the door in her face. She could not believe the bad luck streak she had for the past two weeks.

Chapter Seventeen

For the next two weeks of school Marley locked herself in her room. She didn't eat and she barely slept. All she did was stare out the window from a distance watching the world move on without her. Each day she moved her chair closer to the window so that she could see more of the world. She watched the people board the bus in the mornings and watched the same people get off at their designated stop. She began making up names for them as if they were characters she created. She went from making up names to making up songs about the people. Those songs went from her head and straight on the walls of her room. She sketched out the peoples lives and made up their daily routines. There was one business savvy man she turned into a womanizer. A beautiful Spanish girl got on the bus every Tuesday and she made her a thief. All these people who probably had normal lives in Marley's eyes they were no better off than she was. She turned these innocent people into monsters because everyday in her room when she looked in the mirror that's all she saw. And what she saw she felt the world saw too. It didn't matter what she thought of herself because she was what the world thought of her.

One night she decided to leave the apartment again. The entire time she was in her room alone she figured out the way to Dre's studio. She replayed her visits over and over and on her wall was a sketched map of directions. She had to see him for she felt he was the only one to save her from the depressive state she was currently in.

She ran the entire way keeping one thing in her vision. The empty restaurant was her mark and she saw it as she turned the corner. His car was parked in the back. She knocked on the door and no one answered at first. Marley figured that maybe they were in a recording session so she waited for 30 minutes before she knocked again. This time someone answered and it was her hero.

"What in the hell are you doing here this time of night?" asked Dre. He barely recognized who she was. She looked as if she walked off the street.

"Dre. I'm depressed. I need to talk to you. Please don't let me leave without explaining things to you." she whimpered.

"What are you talking about Marley?"

"I need to talk to you about the concert. You know the one I missed."

"What concert? Ay fellas. Do y'all remember any concert this chick's talking about?" he asked the guys in the studio. "Look I don't know what you are talking about. What do you want?"

"Dre I need you. Please let me come in?" she begged him.

"Oh you need me now that you are looking a hot mess! Man what happened to you. And how did you get here. You know nobody's supposed to know about this spot." He yelled hurting her feelings even more.

"I walked. No I ran to see you," said Marley.

Dre began to laugh. He couldn't believe what she turned into within such a short period of time.

"Look Marley I can't let you in right now. I have an important recording session going on with some important people. I'll catch up with you later. Ok," he said trying to close the door but she pulled with all her strength to keep it open.

"Marley don't start this. Just go on about your business and stop with this crazy stuff now."

He closed the door and for 30 minutes straight she kicked and screamed. Finally he came outside but not to her rescue.

"If you don't leave Marley I swear to God you are going to wish you did! Now leave my premises before I call the cops!" he yelled at her.

"Call them Dre! How could you do this to me! You left me out here all alone in this world. You played with my feelings and let me down. I was only using you any way to get what I wanted. I just wanted to get a deal and I was going to leave your dumb ass. Cause I can do it without you!" she cried hysterically. She didn't mean a word she said but it was too late the damage was done.

Dre was furious-so furious he taught her a lesson he always told her when they were together-don't mess with him or play him when it came to business. Since the concert passed he was going to let everything pass too but Marley just pushed a button that caused Dre to remember what she did to him.

From out of nowhere came 3 police cars with lights flashing on Marley. She was afraid of what was to come.

"Officer she has been banging on my door screaming loud and I am trying to handle business in my business. Can you please have her removed from the premises," said Dre to the female officer.

The officer approached Marley to question her about what was going on and that's when Marley began screaming and crying "Dre I love you! How could you do this to me? I swear if you don't let me in I will kill myself like I've tried to so many times. I am so hurt right now! Please listen to me Dre!" The officers grabbed Marley to handcuff her and she put up a fight kicking and screaming as they put her in the car. She wasn't headed for the precinct but for the hospital because of the words she let flow from her heart through her mouth. Dre and his business partners watched as Marley cried in the car. It hurt him to see his fallen star. The same star that could've outshined the sun had fallen short of her true destiny.

Chapter Eighteen

"Marley you can't keep doing this to yourself," said her mother as she watched her daughter in tears. Her parents couldn't believe what happened to their daughter. They didn't even know half of the story and she was sure to continue to hide it from them. Before they came to visit she cleared her room of all the evidence of her so-called singing career and of her past. She even wore a long sweater to cover up the marks on her arm where she would cut Dre's name in herself.

"Where did we go wrong Marley? Will you please talk to mama?" Her mother took the blame and that's what Marley wanted. Marley wasn't ready to take the blame for her unfortunate mishaps over the past year.

"Do you want to come home soon? Your father and I can arrange that if you like?" asked her mother. She was talking to a once beautiful girl now in a zombie like state of mind. Marley didn't respond to anything her mother said.

"You are still beautiful in mama's eyes." Her mother couldn't stand to see her daughter this way. "You know Marley before Mama died she told me to give you this but I felt you were too young to understand. It's Mama's journal she kept since she had your father. Here you read it when you get down," said her mother as she handed the journal to Marley. It was old and flimsy with the pages folded on the ends and some of the pages torn and out of place. Marley pressed the button for the nurse to come get her mother. She couldn't stomach to sit in her mother's presence any longer.

"Ma'am what do you mean she wants me gone. She can barely think for herself" yelled her mother.

"I'm sorry but the patients have rights and she is of age. You can check with the front desk for more information Mrs. Sheppard," said the nurse as she closed Marley's door. Her mother was furious and when Marley looked up, she thought she saw her grandmother staring through the window of the door. It scared her and when she blinked, it was her mother watching her daughters' life wither to pieces just like the flimsy journal of life her grandmother left for her.

Chapter Nineteen

Marley had been in the ward for four months and according to her she was getting better but to the world she was almost out of breath. She continued to write songs that she thought would be great hits but one day something hit her hard. She was sitting in her room reminiscing on her life at home when she realized she failed. She remembered Damien asking one thing of her-to get her song on the radio so that he could hear her. The entire time Marley was in Chicago she gave life to everyone's dream except for the one person that she held close to her heart. She came to Chicago with one goal besides the one her family thought she was achieving. Within that short period of time Marley did the opposite of what she promised Damien. She began hearing her grandmother's words over and over "you are so smart and that's your weakness." She tried to outsmart everyone through manipulation but it only came back to haunt her. As she stared in the mirror she realized she deceived Damien in several ways. She gave her loyalty to someone else. She was greedy because when it came to her music she only thought of herself. She pushed the wrong people away instead of using them to benefit her in the future. Marley recognized while staring at herself in the mirror that she created a life of fantasies. She created the life instead of living the life. She began crying as she understood that with a blink of an eye she became everyone's worst nightmare.

"Marley you have a visitor" said the nurse. She arose from her bed to see who was in the waiting room. It was Dre. She was excited to see him. Dre meant a lot to Marley in so many ways and she felt she understood him more than ever since they had been a part. He watched Marley reach for stars she was unable to catch. It was like a cat and mouse game. She chased a dream that she was unable to achieve and finally Dre knew it.

Marley was an extremist and that's what kept Dre pushing her more. But what he failed to realize was that Marley didn't stop until it was really over. He appreciated the extreme measures Marley took to make sure he knew who she was in and out. There were only two people that Marley gave her all to and Dre was one of them. She messed up when she gave Dre her mind. It was impossible for Marley to belong to two people. It was impossible for Marley to please two people. And that's why she lived a fantasy filled life. There were two kings in her castle-Dre and Damien.

She never grasped the concept of obedience and loyalty and it was this reason she failed her mission for Damien. She was too extreme for Dre and that is why her dreams never became reality. Marley was too blinded to realize that she was winning a race that everyone quit. She was running this race alone. With all the thoughts running through Marley's head she realized the competition was in her mind only. She was tired at this point and the finish line seemed too far ahead even though the entire time it was so close. Had she stayed focused as her mother reiterated to her several times someone would have joined the race with her to challenge her, to strengthen her and help her endure. Thinking she could do things her way and no other way was the reason Marley was at the ending point of her race. She called all the shots and all this time she thought she had the upper hand through deception.

Before she went outside to see Dre she combed her hair, put on her earrings and straightened up herself. She always thought she had to be a beauty queen for him. She did this because she wanted him to know that she would go to any measure to make him happy but at this point it didn't matter. She gathered up her songs for him and walked out to the waiting area.

"Dre I am so glad you came to see me today. I got something for you. I wrote three new songs today. Today."

"Today?!" Dre replied "Oh that's real good Marley. You look like you're getting better. How are you Ma?" he asked.

"I'm fine now that you are here. It's just I want you to know that I'm doing all I can to get out of here." she cried to him. Marley put herself there and that's why she wasn't getting out any time soon.

She was upset with the world but Marley made her own decisions. She had no right blaming the world for where she was today. She lost her friends, family, and most importantly her dreams. She finished nothing but started everything. That's all she was from the get go...someone who manipulated fantasies. She had Damien thinking she was going to get her song on the radio for him. She had Dre thinking it was worth all the time he put into her to make her a star. She had Felicia thinking she was trustworthy and a good friend. She had her parents thinking she was in school focused on becoming a music teacher. Even Destiny believed she was just that girl. She had everyone thinking what they wanted to think. The only thing was when she couldn't make everyone's fantasy a reality, they became her nightmares. At this point, she could barely decipher her own life.

"Well listen Ma. You know I got mad love for you but I can't be there to save you every time you fall victim of yourself," said Dre as he shook his head looking around at the different people in the room.

"Dre I want this so bad and I feel like this is our year. You are the only who has had my back thus far so please don't walk out on me now." she pleaded with Dre.

"Look I ain't going anywhere. That reminds me I got something for you to listen to," he said as he handed her the CD.

"Who is this?" Marley asked.

"It's one of my new artists who just got signed to major label. And guess who did all the production?"

With her mouth and eyes wide open Marley said, "For Real Dre. Stop playing."

"Look on the back of the cover," said Dre.

"Daammmnnn!" said Marley in disbelief. "So what about my songs. Do you like them? Do I need to change anything? I've been working on them all day. Can we set up a session? Tell me what to do," she said hysterically. With a sympathetic look and five seconds of awkward silence Dre turned and said to her, "Look I gotta go take care of some business. I'll be visiting you soon. You know I can't stay too long because I don't like to see you like this. Remember to redeem yourself to the world and not let the world redeem you. Give me a hug before I go"

She was so happy that Dre came to see her. He put her mind at ease and with his encouraging words Marley was determined she was going to do her best. She decided to play the CD Dre gave her. As she listened she enjoyed the soulful tunes of the young lady on the CD. She has a very beautiful voice Marley thought to herself. She skipped the song and went to the next track. The more she listened to CD the more the songs begin to sound familiar. She sat and listened hard. As she closed her eyes she could see herself in the studio recording the songs she was listening to. She started to hum to the beat of the songs and before she knew it she was harmonizing with the girl on the CD.

Immediately Marley ran to her room to grab her notebook she kept her songs in. She went back to visitor's room and just as she suspected the girl on the CD was singing the very same songs Marley wrote. Marley was distraught by what she hearing. The very same songs she worked hard to write and perfect for Dre someone else was singing. As she walked over to the window she noticed Dre kissing a female in his car. He parked directly in front of her view. It was almost like he wanted her to see who she could've been had she followed Dre's lead.

Marley began to panic. She didn't know whether she should run to him or not. She could not believe her eyes. Dre had already moved on to help another star shine. How could he do this to me? He had me all psyched up thinking I was supposed to ultimately be his successful star. Marley wished that she could be the girl in the car and she was disappointed by what she saw. She began thinking that she was not meant to be with anyone. She found a girl in Damien's bedroom and now she sees Dre kissing a girl in his car.

"This is beginning to be too much for me," she said to herself. Marley feelings of love begin to turn into feeling of regret and as she stood there in the window she realized that her art of fantasy was creating false hopes for others especially those who tried to assist her. She never realized that she had Dre in so many ways. She appreciated him very much but the thought of him allowing someone to make it on her behalf crushed her. The more she stood in the window looking at Dre and his new found love the angrier she became. Marley began to scream. In a rage she broke the CD in half and pressed the sharp edges against her face. Crying hysterically she screamed out "why me? Why me?" Scaring the other patients Marley immediately fell on the floor bleeding profusely, singing one of her songs as if she had an arena full of fans. "See Dre I told you I could do it. I told you I was going to make you proud. Is my tune right? Are we recording? Turn that up? Are my levels right? What about my adlibs?" Marley asked as if her studio session just began. "Can you hear me Dre? Can you hear me?" yelled Marley. Pushing the sharp edges of the blood covered CD she took a deep breath and cut her wrist. It seemed like the same breath she took when she first arrived in the big city.

Chapter Twenty

A few hours later after everything was a little calm a young man approached the counter to say he was visiting Marley.

"What's your name sir and who are you here to visit?" asked the nurse.

"My name is Damien and I am here to visit Marley Sheppard." It was Damien coming to see her. "What happened up here and is everything ok?" he asked.

"Sir will you come in the office with me for a few minutes" asked the nurse as she led him to her office. "I am afraid I have some bad news. Marley passed away about an hour ago. She had a visitor come and see her but something made her snap. We have notified her family. I am sorry about your loss," said the nurse as she gave Damien a few minutes to digest the news. He couldn't believe it. He wondered what happened to her in such a short period to time.

Marley Denise Sheppard never mastered the art of fantasy. She fixed one of her problems and it was her last problem she would ever have to worry about it again. Marley was a mere figment of her own imagination. She capitalized on someone else's ways and made them work for herself but she never conquered one her weakness-her intelligence. She didn't give life a second chance as she gave up her dreams in a city she vowed to conquer and in a world she allowed to dangerously redeem her innocence. She was no longer there to breath in the Chicago air, lay tracks in the studio, study with her friends and party with her roommates. Marley's destiny was in her hands but she decided to take the cheap way out to avoid her true destiny-SELF DESTRUCTION.

About the Author

Tamika Lavette Shuler walks in a passion inspired by her mother and grandmother; a true gift from God-Teaching & Inspiring others to reach higher in life. Having received her degree in English from Benedict College, she slowly but surely found her way back doing what she loved best after working in a corporate position. Her passion for writing stems from her God-given experiences in life. She looks to soar as an inspirational speaker for women and young girls. If you would like to book an engagement to have the author as one of your guest speakers please feel free to send an email to request more information or you may visit her website, www.tamikashuler.com for upcoming events.

A Note From the Author

I hope you enjoyed meeting a piece of me, a creation I love dearly. At some point in our lives we've experienced or met a Marley Denise Sheppard. Maybe not in this same environment but some of the same characteristics. It's amazing how we allow people, places and things change the direction of our lives. I've experienced this deeply in a past relationship and was even at the edge of mental and physical suicide. I allowed someone too deep into my personal circle-my mind. Each of us has a personal circle called our mind. When you allow anyone or anything that does not belong to enter into your most gentle place it can take a major toll on your inner self. Young ladies, be sure to feed your spirit with positive thoughts and surround yourself with soaring eagles. My pastor often tells us that "you can't fly with eagles hanging around turkeys."

You can also think of Marley in terms of our journey to success. Sometimes we don't have enough faith in ourselves to climb the next step of the success ladder. The easy way out seems comes in the form of being content with impassionate duties instead of stepping out on the faith of God's will. It took me a long time to get project Marley rolling and it was not easy. I too was afraid of everyone's opinion and one day I realized it didn't matter what everyone thought. My passion is writing and encouraging women to be strong in all areas of life. Ponder your purpose, develop a plan, and wait on the Lord! If cooking is your passion, cook on sistah! Like Marley, if singing is your passion then sing on sistah! You have to get to the place in life where you are not afraid of the next step, whether it's the stepping stone or success itself!

Remember the puzzle you had as a child. The pieces of it were scattered everywhere on the floor. Each piece uniquely shaped to fit another. It took determination and clear vision to see each piece put together. Each piece brought you closer to the finished product. From a distance they all looked the same but close up you knew that certain pieces just did not fit in certain places. That's how we should view our life. Allow God to give you the vision to the pieces of you life. As you begin to put the puzzle together of your hearts desires watch for the finished product to be a beautiful piece of art. Seek God in all you do. Allow God to be your sense of direction. Cast your cares on Him for His promises will never fail in our lives. Step out on faith! Remember, that which doesn't kill you will make you stronger!

May you be fabulously blessed!
Tamika Lavette Shuler

Memories Marley Left Behind

A Letter from Mama Sheppard before she died

Marley Dee,

I pray this note from Mama finds you in good health. Everything back home is fine but we really do miss you. Grandma had to go to the Dr a few days ago. Don't worry though. You know how I am with my sugar. I know you are making Grandma proud but you know I worry about you a lot. Things in my spirit just tell me the water maybe a little troubled for you. You have to call me and let me know how you are doing and if you need to talk to me just open your mouth. I know you can do that especially with that beautiful voice you got. Marley I love you with all my heart and I just want you to do your best. You deserve to be a successful young lady. I tell you over and over to stay focused on your goals and your dreams will come true but you have to believe that. The moment you stop believing is the moment you loose focus. And when your focus is gone so are your dreams. You call me if you need me. I love you.
Mama Sheppard

A Letter from Marcus after the party

Marley,

I tried to come to you but I was denied three times. Why don't you want to see me? I have done nothing to you. It's hard for me to see you like that. I don't know this person you've become but I want to get to know you so that I can be there for you. I think about you all the time and reminisce on the good times we had but I realized one day you changed overnight. And I don't know why but Marley you are letting life pass you by and pushing the people that matter away. I'm not going anywhere no matter how bad you treat me. I know you can be the Marley I met on campus and the Marley who blew the audience away last fall. You may be the last one standing to the world but you're still the best one left to me. Save the best for last and to me that's you. You need to let the world see who you can be, the girl I know and the girl I love no matter what. I hope to see you soon Marley. Please let me in....one day.

Marcus

Fly with Me

Verse One

What is this feeling got me going insane
They say I'm crazy 'cause I'm calling his name
I see you staring trying to figure me out
I'm looking back like what's this all about
I'm saying move but you're saying please stay
Fighting these feelings steady pushing away
My mind is racing and life's passing me by
Now you're holding out your hand saying please come
and fly with me

Chorus
Baby I believe you see something else in me that my eyes
can't see but heart still beats for his love
(Repeat with I believe)

It's so amazing how you call me your lady
But all I hear is when he calls me his baby
I'm holding on to his feelings so strong b/c my life can't
go on without him
He knows me and he believes in me and I don't deserve
you because I know I'll hurt you
Now you're staring in my face saying come back to my
place with me

Chorus
Baby I believe you see something else in me that my eyes
can't see but heart still beats for his love
(Repeat with I believe)

Bridge

What can you do for me I can't go with you

I gotta walk away
And you're saying stay
I know I'll hurt you and when he calls I will desert you
I can't waste your time boy maybe in the next life time

Chorus
You can fly with me but baby I believe he'll redeem himself to me cause my heart still bleeds for his love